Duncan,

Son of Sagira

By

E.C. Holley

FIVE FROM ONE

THREE DAUGHTERS AND TWO SONS

ONE WITH FIRE

ONE WITH SIGHT

ONE TO TELL YOU WRONG FROM RIGHT

ONE TO HIDE

ONE TO RUN

EACH WITH THE GOLDEN POWER OF THE SUN

.

For the love of my life,
Brian

TABLE OF CONTENTS

PART ONE

Chapter 1

Nellie had no business becoming a mother, and she knew it.

3 a.m. Six little hearts were beating rapidly inside her. It was time.

Collapsing onto her worn-out bed, Nellie hooked her claws into her threadbare flannel blanket and braced for the next contraction.

Hold on little ones, she breathed into the night.

Nellie rearranged the blanket and her body to block the chill of the early morning. Damp air from an open window clung to her hot face. She could delay no longer. Feeling the life inside her stirring, Nellie took a deep breath, opened her round golden eyes, and pushed.

The first kitten to be born was a lean, dark brown tabby. She protested as Nellie cleaned her with her coarse tongue. *Hello, Anna,* Nellie whispered as she cradled her daughter against her warm body.

Focusing on the rhythmic pattern of the rain falling outside, Nellie pushed again, then gently examined her second child. She was light grey and speckled with white, as if she had fallen face first into a bowl of cream. *Hello, Sara.* Sara wrinkled her pink nose and mewed softly at her mother.

Laying her head back down, Nellie smiled to reassure herself, *Four more.*

Exhausted, Nellie welcomed her twins. Holding fast to each other, the girls struggled as their mother cleaned their long matted fur. *Hello Kate, Hello Emma.* Nellie gave a tired sigh and looked down at her four daughters. *Two more,* she murmured. *Make room for your brothers.*

Nellie grimaced as she gave birth to her first son. He was much larger than his sisters with serious grey whiskers that contrasted sharply against his newborn face. *Hello, Theo,* she lifted him carefully between her teeth and placed him on a dry part of the blanket.

Almost. Nellie felt her body contract sharply once again. Tensing her jaw, she gathered the strength to push for the last time that night.

But the sixth... the sixth was different.

Nellie's golden eyes flashed with alarm.

Several minutes passed as she stared down at her son. He was identical to his mother, all black with just a small patch of white cutting a diamond on his chest. Feeling her breath on his newborn body, he turned toward her. As his blind eyes met hers, Nellie stopped. Her body tensed, and her son began to cry, pulling himself toward her. As he clutched her, she went limp, yielding to the knowledge that she had already failed him. *Hello, Duncan,* she whispered sadly. Nellie let her smooth black nose touch her son's. *Oh, my dear child, I am so very sorry.* She began to lick gently behind his ear. *I did not mean this life for you.*

Chapter 2

Eight Weeks Later

We know the rules, Anna! Sara swished her gray tail and twitched her cream-tipped whiskers with impatience. *We race all the time.*

Still! Anna shifted her glare to her brother, *Some of us could use a reminder!*

Duncan smiled, his black whiskers curled with amusement. *I can't help it if I'm faster than you, Sis. Maybe you should have asked Mom for racing stripes,* he laughed, ducking to avoid a swipe from his sister's paw. Losing his balance, Duncan fell back into the arms of his mother.

Nellie popped Duncan on the nose with her tail. *Be nice to your sister, Duncan!*

Mom! Mom! Will you watch? pleaded Kate and Emma.

Nellie nuzzled her twin daughters, *I'll be right over here on the couch.*

Let's go! grumbled Theo.

Right, Anna interrupted. *We start at the LEGOS, over the couch, around the lamp, military-crawl under the TV, up and over the laundry basket, three times around the ficus tree, and the foosball table is the finish line.*

Mom, you keep watch.

Yes, dear. All right, children, line up. Nellie leapt onto the arm of the couch and smiled down at her children. *One, two... I see that paw, Sara... three, Go!*

Nellie tried to hide her laughter, but she couldn't help but chuckle watching her six little ones run around the basement. They were improving rapidly, but their uncoordinated limbs left them resembling a herd of frenzied hamsters rather than a pack of agile feline predators.

Poor Theo, so competitive and strong, but certainly not built for speed. He had yet to outgrow his kitten fat, and his belly swung from side to side as he struggled to keep up with Emma and Kate.

Anna was leaner and darker than her three sisters, and both she and Sara were incredibly fast. The only difference was that Sara ran with such joy, you could feel it surge in her gait, while Anna ran only with steadfast determination to beat her dark-furred little brother.

Duncan, the only boy beside Theo, was faster than all the others, more agile, more powerful. And he always won, always.

Nellie watched as Duncan did a victory dance under the foosball table, his little kitten butt swishing from side to side, making Sara laugh and Anna hiss.

You only went two and a half times around the ficus tree, Duncan! That win doesn't count! I want a rematch! Anna growled.

6

Theo gasped, *I'm breathing like a flat-faced Persian over here, Anna! Give us a minute!*

Anna rolled her eyes at the sight of her wheezing brother. *Fine, you can have five whole minutes, Theo. I'll be over here stretching.*

Good one, Duncan, said Sara as she licked her brother playfully across the cheek.

Duncan flashed his baby teeth into a grin and lowered his voice so that only Sara could hear. *I just like watching Anna freak out.*

Me too, smiled Sara, looking over at her sister feverishly stretching out her haunches, *Me too.*

Duncan trotted over to where his mother sat perched on the couch. He stretched up on his hind legs to bat at her swishing tail. His sharp kitten claws stuck in the soft suede, making popping sounds as he pulled them out one at a time. Smiling, Duncan hopped up onto the plush couch to join her. He plopped down on the center cushion, rolling onto his back, his black belly fur fluffing out every which way. He loved the way his arms and legs burned after a good race. Nellie tickled his belly with her tail, and Duncan laughed, flopping back onto his stomach.

His siblings soon followed. Sara leapt after her brother while Kate and Emma secured a few claw-holds before dragging themselves up. Theo's extra weight caused the cushion to dip, rolling his brother and sisters back into him. Theo laughed and gently placed a paw on Duncan's forehead.

Not to be outdone, even in the realm of cuddling, Anna placed herself squarely on top of the makeshift kitten mountain. *Five minutes,* she mumbled sleepily. *Mom, make sure to wake us up.*

Nellie smiled down at the mass of fat, fur, and angelic faces that were still visible.

Yes, dear, she said softly, *five minutes.*

~

Two Hours Later

Mom! How could you let us oversleep? I said five minutes! Anna jumped up and down on the couch cushion, forcing her siblings to roll off, tumbling every which way. *All right, everyone line up!* she roared.

Nellie raised her eyebrow whiskers incredulously at her first born child. *Anna, honey, I'm not sure this is a good idea. It's almost bedtime.* Theo, Emma, and Kate nodded solemnly with their mother, still groggy from their nap and hoping to get out of losing another obstacle course forced on them by their overly competitive siblings.

Please, Mom? begged Anna. Nellie frowned. She never thought she'd be such a pushover, and yet here she was. *All right, but only those who want to race--no bullying your brother and sisters!*

Anna rolled her eyes. *Fine, fine. Sara, Duncan, and me.* Duncan and Sara exchanged playful glances. Anna glared at her siblings, her dark tabby stripes furrowing into a deep "M" over her brow.

Nellie let out a heavy sigh and signaled for Kate, Emma, and Theo to watch from their bed. The familiar, flannel-lined cardboard box was situated in a dark corner of the basement. Nellie took her place on top of the couch to officiate, and the three kittens settled down into the folds of the flannel to watch their siblings.

While Anna felt along the cold basement tile for the best claw hold,

Duncan nudged Sara, licked both paws, and slicked back his whiskers. Sara gave him a mock serious face and took her spot beside Anna. The three kittens looked expectantly at their mother.

Nellie raised her tail and began the countdown. *One, two, three, Go!*

She watched as they began tearing around the house. As usual, Duncan pulled easily ahead of his sisters. Nellie shook her head. She had been watching these last eight weeks, waiting, hoping that she was wrong.

Her mind drifted back to the night of his birth and what she had seen in his sightless blue kitten eyes that had filled her with such dread. Duncan was one of the chosen, and Nellie could no longer pretend otherwise. She had doomed her child to a life of secrecy, pain, and profound loneliness. From the white diamond on his chest to his long dark whiskers, looking at him was like looking at her own reflection. *You are the son of my body and the brother of my fate,* she whispered sadly.

As Duncan raced easily up and over the laundry basket, he paused to smile at his mother, meeting her great yellow eyes with his. Then, without warning, he lurched forward and collapsed, hitting the tile hard with his body. His vision began to narrow, going gray, then fading to black. He went rigid and seized. In his mind he was trying to run, but his body was shutting down. His eyes darted back and forth, and his muscles contracted slowly. The sounds around him became muffled and distorted until there was only silence. The world began to skip. Images flashed through his brain, horrible images. He howled a guttural cry so agonized and filled with terror that it raised the hairs on the backs of every one of his siblings. Sara skidded to a stop, claws scratching and grappling on the tile as she tried to slow herself.

No! Duncan cried, stuck in his waking nightmare. *Stop, Anna! The table... Stop!* He yowled desperately, eyes horrified, still unable to control his limbs. *No cheating, Duncan! You tripped,* Anna cried over her shoulder. She sped up, heading straight for the foosball table, *I'm winning this one!* With a loud crack, the foosball table's right leg snapped, crashing to the floor with a deafening thud. Duncan watched as his sister fell under the weight of the table. He could hear the cries of his siblings.

Slowly, shapes began to emerge from out of the darkness.

He looked for his mother. She was gone from her place on the couch.

Anna... she was still running!

Duncan struggled to raise his head, disoriented and nauseous. He watched the table crash again. Only this time, his mother stood holding a trembling little tabby by the scruff of the neck, a safe five feet from the remains of the table.

The kittens raced to their mother and their still trembling sister. *Are you okay?* squeaked Emma. *What happened?* whimpered Kate. *I saw Duncan fall and then the table, how?* cried Theo. Sara held her cream-colored paw up to her mother, speechless.

Nellie set Anna down carefully, releasing her tight hold on her daughter's neck.

Quiet! Everyone to bed! She hissed. *Now!*

Duncan pulled himself up slowly from the ground. *No.* His arms and legs were still shaking.

The other kittens stared at him. Duncan had always been a bit of a dare-devil and troublemaker, but he had never boldly defied their mother.

Mom, I saw it. I saw the table fall on Anna. She was hurt...

What? stammered Sara.

I don't know... I just saw... I did... Duncan's voice grew urgent.

Enough! growled Nellie.

No! I saw! You saw it too! I know you did! You saw it, and you stopped it!

The five kittens watched Duncan's shaking body with frightened eyes. Nellie lowered her face, her beautiful, elegant face, down to Duncan's, and her fierce yellow eyes silenced him. She firmly pointed her tail in the direction of their bed, and the six kittens followed. Only Duncan moved more slowly.

~

As the last of his siblings fell asleep, Duncan carefully crawled out of bed and approached his mother. Her yellow eyes moved methodically, scanning the room, focusing on the sliding-glass door. Nellie's tail twitched nervously, and she sat stiffly, like a night guard at her post.

Mom?

Yes, dear, Nellie spoke quietly with no hint of surprise in her voice. Duncan paused. He was expecting her to be angry. He cleared his throat and whispered. *Something happened to me today.*

Nellie exhaled heavily. *I know.*

Duncan could hear the fear and sadness in her voice. He moved closer to his mother.

I saw... I saw that table fall, and... I saw Anna... Duncan stopped, too frightened by what he had seen to continue. *I looked for you, and you had already moved her.*

Nellie kept her eyes fixed on their reflection in the sliding-glass door. She waited. Choosing her words carefully, she lowered her voice. *We are different, Duncan.*

I don't understand, he whispered, his bright blue eyes distant, troubled.

Nellie looked down at her son, her eyes full of guilt, for reasons Duncan could not yet understand. *You and I, we are special. I have known from the moment you were born. I had hoped...* she paused again... *Duncan, you and I can do things, see things, that other cats can't even imagine. Today was just the beginning. I have kept this a secret from you,* Nellie raised her head to resume looking out the window. *I thought... I had hoped that I was wrong.* She sighed again. *I am sorry for that. I should have told you before today.*

Duncan's eyes burned, flashing like a hot blue flame against his deep black fur. *Then tell me now. Tell me what is happening to me.*

Tomorrow, replied Nellie firmly, *tomorrow.*

Duncan began to protest, but after one look at his mother's hard face, he realized that no amount of arguing would do any good. What he had seen happen to Anna, the horrible thing that could have happened to Anna, his mother had also seen. It was replaying over and over in her mind, too. As he turned to join his siblings, sleeping soundly in their warm bed, he decided to risk asking one more question.

Mom?

Yes, Duncan? she lowered her golden eyes to meet his gaze.

How did you know I was like you? I mean, you said you've known since the day I was born. How did you know?

Nellie held her son's stare. *I saw your eyes.*

What do you mean? What's special about my eyes?

Not your eyes now. Nellie raised her paw to smooth her son's dark fur. *You and your brother and sisters will have blue eyes while you are young, but as you grow and change, so will the color of your eyes. Even now, they are changing.* She stopped. How do you begin to explain the impossible, she asked herself sadly. *I have seen your brother's and sisters' eyes. They will be like your father's--emerald green, outlined in black.* Nellie took a step back toward her post. *I saw your eyes too, Duncan. I saw the eyes of who you would become, the eyes of who, of what, you are.*

Duncan moved forward and sat quietly alongside his mother, following her gaze. He could see their soft reflection in the sliding-glass door. Two sets of eyes stared back at him.

Nellie turned her head away so that she could no longer see their reflection. In a tired whisper she answered her son's unspoken question.

They were bright gold, Duncan, just like mine.

Chapter 3

Duncan curled one paw over his eyes as the morning light streamed through the entrance to their cardboard bed. His head ached and he still felt slightly nauseous. His stomach gurgled and he scratched it with his back paw. He must be hungry.

Duncan lifted his dew-claw to peer out at the early morning. He yawned, arched his back, and inhaled deeply. He was the last of his siblings to wake. This was unusual as he was normally the first to rise each morning.

Stumbling slightly, Duncan made his way up the ramp to the large beige dome that was their litter box. The kittens had been exposed to human television and movies in their eight weeks of life, and in that short time, Duncan had developed a love for science-fiction. He couldn't help but think his bathroom resembled a very small, very stinky space ship. He found this idea endlessly entertaining, and he liked to pretend he was being called to the command center whenever he had to go to the bathroom. Wrinkling his nose, he found his way to an acceptable corner of the litter box dome, assumed the position of captain, and began to think.

He couldn't be *that* different from his siblings, could he? What was all this talk about him being special? Duncan could feel his stomach contract in a wave of nausea. He stood hunched over in the litter box, overcome by the need to vomit all over his imaginary command center.

Nellie peeked her head into the box, *You okay in there, Duncan?*

Yeah, Mom, a little privacy please? Nellie made a skeptical face but pulled her head back out of the box.

So he sensed something bad was going to happen. So what? Maybe he and his mother just happened to see the table leg crack before the others. Maybe Anna was just lucky and that was all there was to it. Who cares what color his eyes were going to be? Lots of cats have yellow eyes. Duncan's stomach convulsed and he vomited what little was left in his stomach. His body shook from the intensity of the lurching.

Seriously, Duncan, do you need some help in there? There's nothing to be ashamed of. Not all kittens find the litter box easy to use in the beginning...

No, really, I'm fine, Mom! Don't come in!

Duncan hastily dug his paws through the sandy litter. As he climbed tentatively out of the box and the fresh air hit his face, he felt the nausea start to pass and the knot in his stomach loosen. He noticed his siblings were all engaged in various games, taking place in a newly confined area. He moved to join them, his spirits lifted. Even his mother's quizzical gaze didn't bother him a bit as he moved with steadfast determination to start his day.

15

Apparently the human family had found the remains of their foosball table when they had arrived home from work and had sentenced the six kittens and their mother to a period of confinement. Where there had once been wide-open space, the human parents had constructed a makeshift wall out of bookshelves, baby gates, and flattened boxes reinforced with concrete blocks. Still, there was a carpet climbing tree, several crinkly paper bags, and a selection of brightly colored mice and rainbow-colored balls to play with.

As he began to head toward the climbing tree, Duncan saw the door crack. All eyes turned to the small human girl carrying two pink plastic plates, each about six inches in diameter, filled with watered-down mush... tasty, meaty, watery mush. Whatever it looked like, it beat milk for every meal.

Theo barreled forward, knocking Kate and Emma out of the way with one swing of his ample hips.

Anna and Sara jumped down from the climbing tree and raced past Duncan with enough speed to blow the remaining litter off his hind legs.

Nellie watched motionless from the corner.

The human child carefully placed the two plates a few feet apart from each other, and the frenzy began. Duncan, who normally led the charge, found himself struggling to break into either circle of feeding siblings. His nausea had been replaced by an intense hunger, yet he was finding it nearly impossible to reach the food.

With Theo being the size of one and a half normal kittens, he and Anna managed to take up an entire plate for themselves. Sara, Kate, and Emma crowded around the second. Each time Duncan tried to insert himself, either his brother or one of his sisters edged him out.

Come on guys, hey, I... I can't get any....

No response.

Sara! Duncan pleaded.

Can't talk, eating, she replied awkwardly, forcing more mush into her mouth.

As the little girl watched, she called for her mother.

"Mom, look how cute, come look!"

The child ran upstairs and before long returned carrying another plate of food. Her mother followed, frantically pushing buttons on her phone.

Duncan watched the girl set a new heaping plate of food down. He approached, waiting to be ambushed by his siblings. Theo, Anna, Sara, Kate, Emma; they all saw the food, Duncan was sure of it, but none of them moved. They simply turned away and continued to eat as if nothing, as if no one, was there.

Duncan looked down at as his plate, letting a small mew escape his mouth.

"Aww, how cute, he's got the whole plate to himself," the girl tugged at her mother's sleeve.

Through the viewing screen on the phone, next to the blinking red dot, the human mother could see the two plates, one on the left, and one on the right, both surrounded by kittens struggling to get their share. In the center, a third plate with a single black kitten, eating his breakfast alone.

~

Only Duncan had yet to finish eating. He ate sloppily, angrily, his front paws in the center of the shallow plastic plate. He continued to eat his way down around his feet, his body crouched, his mouth working wildly.

Nellie approached him, a disapproving expression on her face.

Duncan, dear, are you done eating yet? They gave you quite a bit more than usual this morning, maybe you should slow down?

Ignoring his mother, Duncan continued to wolf down his breakfast. Fine, he thought to himself, if they don't want to eat with me, I'll eat by myself... I'll eat the whole dish... I'll....

Duncan's internal rant was interrupted by the human girl as she picked up his food dish from under his paws.

"I know, Mom! I'm going! I know they'll be here soon!" she yelled back up the stairs. The door slammed and the kittens could hear a series of thuds as the girl raced back up to her mother.

Duncan stood there exposed, his front paws wet and covered in chicken-flavored paste, his chin coated with a thin layer clumping in the center such that he appeared to be sporting a cat-food goatee.

Oh, Duncan! scolded Nellie. *We are civilized kittens here! Eating like a four-week-old?* she chided him, grooming him with rapid precision and skill, the kind of damage control only mothers are capable of.

Licking her own whiskers satisfactorily, Nellie let out a sigh, *There!* Duncan was at least presentable for company now. *Go play with your brother and sisters until it is time for our visitors.*

Fine, fine, Duncan muttered, slightly embarrassed to have been groomed so forcefully and thoroughly by his mother in front of his siblings. Oh well, maybe the chance to make fun of him might help distract them from yesterday's events, or at least get them to talk to him.

Anna and Sara had returned to the climbing tree while Theo, Kate, and Emma were leading an excavation of one of the brown paper bags.

Duncan decided to approach the trio of explorers first.

Hey, guys! Duncan said with added enthusiasm. *What are you up to?*

Theo responded seriously, *We're excavating this cave, Duncan.* He sounded slightly annoyed, as if this fact should have been obvious.

While Duncan had watched a great deal of science-fiction television in the past eight weeks, Theo had watched even more hours of Discovery and History channel specials. Duncan stopped and waited while his brother tried to squeeze through a hole in the paper bag. It ripped as he pulled his belly through.

Kate and Emma will be assisting me, said Theo, adding a slight British accent to his voice.

Cool... replied Duncan, drooping his whiskers, trying (but failing) to look as interested as Theo. *Can I play, or, er, help?* asked Duncan, changing "play" to "help" as he observed Theo's serious gray brow turn even more skeptical.

Uh, you can assist Kate and Emma.

What? Last week you said I could be a rival historian excavating Cave B!

Theo shifted uncomfortably, clearly not wanting to continue this exchange with his brother any longer than necessary. *The girls need assistance this week. Follow their trail, you'll see.*

Duncan sighed and followed the trail of white fluff leading to the back corner of the paper bag.

Kate waved her paw, pointing her claw to a sliced-open pink plush mouse lying motionless on the ground. *We're dissecting mice!*

Emma elbowed her dim-witted sister. *It's a mummy, Kate. A mummy.*

Theo said you guys needed assistance today, mumbled Duncan.

Emma looked nervously over at Kate, only to find she was still preoccupied with the fake mouse guts she had strewn across the floor.

Um, I think we're okay, Duncan. Emma shifted awkwardly, not wanting to make eye contact with her brother.

Theo pretended to be busy deciphering some claw marks on the walls of the bag while Kate and Emma continued to poke at the gutted toy mouse.

Fine, I guess I'll see what Sara and Anna are doing, muttered Duncan, trying to hide the disappointment and hurt in his voice as he exited the imaginary cave.

Duncan made his way toward Sara and Anna, who were busy climbing on the large carpeted cat tree.

Hey, guys.

Anna gave him her usual gruff nod, but at least Sara smiled at him.

Hi, Duncan, she replied tentatively, clearly trying to erase the strange events of yesterday from her mind.

Do you guys want to play? asked Duncan.

Surely, Anna wouldn't refuse a climbing competition, but before either sister could reply, Nellie interrupted.

Quickly! Over here, quickly children!

As all the kittens gathered around their mother, Nellie's voice dropped to a low whisper.

We're having visitors. Now remember the rules. What is the first rule again?

The kittens replied in unison.

1. We must never display any unusual behavior in front of the humans.

Such as? prompted Nellie.

Emma raised her paw eagerly to answer. *Yes, Emma.*

We must never do any of the following... high five during sporting events, laugh or cry during movies, read books or magazines, play on the computer, have intelligent conversation with each other, and so forth.

Very good, Emma.

And what is the second rule? drilled Nellie.

The kittens replied again in unison.

2. We must let the humans think they are smarter than us.

All right, they're coming, said Nellie quietly. *Take your positions.*

She turned to face the door and scolded herself for wasting so much time trying to avoid the inevitable. She whispered under her breath, *There is never enough time.*

~

The door opened and the human parents entered, followed by their daughter and a young married couple. They had visited a few times before. They were both nice, with rosy round faces, and if you worked your way into their belly fat, you sunk down nicely.

The human man was extremely tall with big feet covered in delightfully large, stinky socks. Duncan couldn't wait to grab onto the man's feet. It was like playing with a foot-long catnip mouse that squealed and squirmed when you bit into it. The human woman had a loud but friendly voice, and she laughed at almost everything the kittens did. While slightly clingy, she was far more gentle and fun to play with than many of their other visitors (most of which had sticky, jelly-flavored, hands and were under the age of 10). Duncan was glad to see it was them who were visiting that day.

As the kittens set about engaging in suitably idiotic behaviors for their human company, Duncan and Sara began to approach the young couple, now seated on the floor.

Nellie watched carefully from the top of the couch. She kept her eyes focused, ready to diffuse any dangerous situations that might arise. She had carried off many a naughty kitten by the scruff of the neck for breaking one of the rules.

The woman had her hands outstretched to both kittens. Duncan mewed out of the side of his mouth so that the humans couldn't tell he was talking to Sara, *This lady always seems a bit desperate for attention, don't you think?* Sara skillfully laughed and mewed back, *I think I'm going to walk with my claws out on this guy's legs. He makes the funniest noises.* Both kittens approached, purring innocently.

It was in that moment, as Duncan's nose touched the hand of the woman, that his body went rigid again, just like it had right before the foosball table leg broke. It was less intense physically, but a clear series of pictures came flooding into his mind. There were so many images this time. They were confusing. What did they mean?

A flash, followed by a dull ache, spread through his jaw to the back of his head.

Suddenly he was in a small room with soft cream carpet that left impressions under his paws as he walked. The door was closed. He did not know this place.

Argh! His head felt like it was splitting in half!

Duncan turned his head and saw two tiny metal bowls, a plastic carrier with a bunch of holes in it, and a litter box. The walls were covered in pictures of the young married couple. He could smell litter and the distinctive aroma of the chicken-flavored mush.

Inside his vision, he turned his head again. He was alone. Where was Sara? Where was his mother? *Where was he?*

And like that, it was gone.

No! shouted Duncan, but as he yelled Nellie knocked off a box of LEGOS sitting on the end table.

While the humans, distracted, rushed to pick up the scattered toys, Nellie dragged her struggling son by the scruff of the neck off to his cardboard-box bedroom.

Mom! yelled Duncan. *I saw something!*

Shhhh, pleaded Sara, her eyes distraught, *don't do this.* She followed quickly along behind her mother. Duncan was making a scene--even by kitten standards.

Duncan fought harder against his mother's grip.

Mom! he yowled.

Duncan! Nellie hissed. *Stop this instant! You have no idea what you're risking!*

Suddenly the images began to come together.

Nellie turned quickly to her daughter. *Sara, go back and wait with Theo and your sisters. Your brother is sick.*

But, Mom? Sara looked at her brother and then back to her mother.

Sara, I need you to go. He'll be fine. Remember the rules. Sara hesitated. Nellie lowered her voice, *I promise he'll be fine, Sara. Go.*

Duncan understood now, he saw everything. These people, this couple, they were going to take him away from his family. His siblings, one by one, they would be taken away... the images, they were all from his life, from his future.

His sisters and his brother had no idea.

As his vision cleared, Duncan took all his fear and all his anger and turned it on his mother. *You said you'd tell me what's happening to me today, so tell me, tell me now! Those people are going to take us, and you...* he let the last few words out slowly, he wanted to make her hurt the way he hurt... *you were going to let them!*

To the human family and their two guests, Nellie appeared to be having a fight with one of her kittens, or rather, her kitten appeared to be trying

24

to have a fight with her. As the human mother came to investigate, Nellie realized the scene they were making.

Tell me the truth! he yelled.

Nellie's eyes turned to within an inch of Duncan's, and they pulsed a magnificent golden yellow. For Duncan, it was like looking directly into the sun.

HUSH!

Duncan's feet buckled from underneath him, and he felt himself falling sharply into unconsciousness. A series of images flashed before him, too fast to understand, but he could have sworn he saw his mother's life flash before his eyes. His vision narrowed.

Nellie placed him under the old flannel blanket that lined their bed. The last thing Duncan could remember hearing was his mother's voice saying...

Tonight then, I guess it will have to be tonight.

And then Duncan heard nothing.

Chapter 4

Duncan felt his mother's tongue running along the bridge of his nose, warm and rough, it pulled like a comb through his fur. He opened his eyes.

It was dark, but he could feel the warmth of his brothers and sisters in the bed next to him. It must be nighttime. How long was he out?

The moonlight streamed into their bed, outlining his mother's face. She was sitting in the dark, watching him. His eyes met hers briefly, and with that, he felt her mouth grab behind his neck and lift him over his siblings.

Nellie carried her son like this as she jumped easily over the human-built wall. Landing lightly, she carefully set Duncan down.

Follow me, she mouthed silently.

Duncan's limbs were stiff, and he walked with difficulty at first, but on the inside he was wide awake. His mind was racing. He had so many questions for her.

Nellie slowed to let her son catch up. *The stiffness in your limbs will pass.*

Duncan thought he had never heard so much sadness in her voice.

I'm sorry, she whispered, *for this morning, for everything.*

Duncan paused. Her words and her guilt felt heavy on his shoulders.

It's okay, Mom. You're going to tell me everything now though, right?

Nellie turned her head toward her son, but she kept her eyes from meeting his. *Yes, Duncan. I'm going to tell you everything, but you must promise to keep everything I tell you tonight a secret. Can you do that?*

Duncan nodded, *Yes.*

Nellie had stopped. They were in a new corner of the house. Nellie thought it resembled a graveyard. It was a storeroom lined with bookshelves filled with games and toys that the human girl no longer wanted. It was a place to be hidden away from the rest of the world, a place to be forgotten... a place to gather dust. Nellie's lips curled into a bittersweet smile. It was not by chance that she chose to bring Duncan here to tell him the same story told to her when she was his age. Nellie looked down at her son. The way he carried himself, the seriousness of his face, it all made him look older than he was. She had seen this day, but she hadn't realized it would come so soon. After tonight, Duncan's life would never be the same. He would always be alone. Deep down she knew that. Deep down she had always hoped she was wrong.

Yes, Mom, I can do that, Duncan repeated, wondering if his mother had heard him the first time.

She had.

Nellie sat down next to a stack of board games and beckoned Duncan to join her.

Alright then, I shall tell you the story of where we come from, the story of our kind, the story of Sagira.

~

Her story begins in ancient Egypt, in the land of pyramids and pharaohs, in the city of Bubastis on the Nile Delta.

Before the time of Sagira, cats were wild. We hunted and lived with those who were like us, and we cared nothing for humans and humans cared nothing for us. But around the time of Sagira, our paths converged, and cats and humans found themselves in a position to help one another. We cats hunted rodents that fed on human grain, and so we earned respect and reverence from the humans. We were even buried alongside them when they died.

But Sagira came and changed everything. Nellie paused for effect. Duncan sat motionless and wide-eyed.

To look at her, one would think she was an ordinary black cat, but Sagira was anything but ordinary. She was the first and most powerful of our kind, but her life was a mysterious one, and what I tell you tonight is all that is and ever will be known about her origins.

Sagira was a small but deadly huntress. It was said that when she would hunt it was as though she would become one with the shadows, invisible except for a pair of perfectly round golden eyes that flashed right before the kill. She was said to have killed so many rodents, their death tally so high, that the mice and rats fled in great numbers from the city to escape the death that was sure to await them if they stayed in the land home to Sagira.

Nellie paused again.

But Sagira could do more than track and kill rodents.

Legend says that in an instant she could burst into flames, become invisible, move faster than the deadliest snake, and even bend minds to her will. They say she could see things before they happened...

Humans were different then, but in some ways they were very much the same. They were driven by superstition and fear, but most of all, by greed. And so one day they witnessed Sagira's powers and believed her to be a goddess. They worshiped her and called her by the name of Bast, the human cat-goddess. They chose her above all others to be the spouse of their creator god, and no doubt because of her ability to burst into flames, they believed she harnessed the power of the sun with her golden eyes.

But the humans could not tell which of us possessed the gifts of Sagira and which did not.

And so all cats were worshipped as gods.

Duncan forced himself to breathe. Nellie continued.

The humans held a festival every year in her honor during which they would drink and indulge in their many vices. The air would hang heavy with smell of spices and the echo of drums. The humans danced and sang songs of their goddess... but their goddess was nowhere to be found.

Sagira had not asked for their songs, and she did not want their worship.

She stayed away from humans and from other cats as best she could. They say her speech became increasingly strange and that she began to have difficulty telling the present from the future. Other cats began to worship her. They followed her wherever she went, recording her every word, even the ones they did not understand. Scribes of Sagira, they were called... keepers of the Book of Sagira.

But as time went on, Sagira began to spend more and more time alone. And one night, she disappeared. Months passed, and no one had seen or heard from Sagira. Then, without warning, she reappeared. But she was no longer the same lonely huntress that had first arrived in Bubastis. She was pregnant.

No one ever knew the name of the father, for Sagira never spoke of him. Some say the time spent out in the wild with her visions drove her mad; others say it was the pain of love that made her the way she was, but Sagira never spoke of her wanderings, not even to her kittens... who became known to our kind as the Five Children of Sagira; three girls and two boys.

Duncan's eye's widened.

Each inherited one of Sagira's five powers, and it has been that way ever since. All were black as night except for the small white diamond on their chest. All had her perfect golden eyes. It is said that Sagira died alone, disappearing one night into the dark, never to be seen again. The children of Sagira scattered, spreading to different corners of the Earth. They bred with other cats, passing on their powers to a small number of descendants.

As more time passed, the humans became fickle toward us--as humans often do. They came to believe our tendency to hunt at night meant that we were one with the devil, that we were possessed by demons, and that we were a weapon of witchcraft and black magic. Their worship of our kind turned to fear, so they chose to punish us.

And so all cats were hunted as demons.

Other cats blamed the descendants of Sagira for their suffering, and they turned on our kind and all those who aligned themselves with us. They believed us to be a danger to the survival of our species. Many of us had become reckless using our powers in front of the humans. In an effort to hunt us, many cats were killed and our kind nearly wiped out. These cats, like the humans, had grown to fear and to hate us. In their desperation, rules for behavior in front of humans were set down to be followed by all cats, the same rules that I have taught to you and your siblings. It was believed that these rules would allow us to live alongside humans again. An elite guard of purebreds, who had not mixed with our kind, were called to act as guardians of the species by hunting down any remaining Children of Sagira and their allies and to enforce the rules of behavior. And yet, in spite of all this, the Scribes of Sagira maintained their devotion. They stayed feral, living off the land, protecting our past by passing their stories and legends from generation to generation... lonely keepers of the Book of Sagira.

Nellie stopped. Her voice grew as dark as the night that surrounded them.

Their support was not enough. We were being hunted from both sides, by humans and cats alike. The world was no longer safe for us. And so, like Sagira, our kind vanished into the night, hiding our powers away from the world.

She looked down at her son.

To this day, the humans consider black cats to be bad luck, cats tell stories of us to scare their kittens, the rules continue to be passed down from mother to child, and we... the Children of Sagira stay hidden, even from our own brothers and sisters. We must never reveal that we are Children of Sagira, and we must never let anyone, human or cat, know of our powers, or it is believed that we will all become hunted again.

~

Duncan sat in silence with his mother for several minutes. Nellie waited.

So you and I... we have?

Nellie's voice grew lighter. *The power of sight, yes, we see things before they happen. You will learn to control your visions with time. You will even learn how to blind others with your visions when you are faced with no other alternative... what I did to you this morning.* Nellie stopped. *The effect was particularly strong on someone of your age. When done to someone without our gifts, however, the effect is even more powerful.*

The room was quiet while Duncan tried to absorb what his mother was saying.

But, what about what I saw... Duncan swallowed hard... *what we saw happen to Anna?*

Nellie looked down at her son. *We see the future.*

Duncan shook his head. *I don't... I don't understand.*

In our visions, we see the future as it is written, but with all of our visions we have a choice... to lead, or to follow, the path in front of us. But Duncan, when we choose to alter the course of fate, we must pay a price.

So you chose to save Anna?

Nellie smiled grimly. *Yes, I chose to save her.*

Duncan sat, deep in thought. *But what cost can there be to that?*

Nellie's voice grew weary. *The cost of losing you, Duncan.*

Duncan tried to form words, but he was speechless.

Nellie spoke softly. *Two of you will stay here with me; the rest of you will be taken far away from here. Our paths will change.*

You mean... you mean they would have kept me... if...

Nellie raised a paw to keep him from finishing.

Duncan could see the exhaustion in his mother's face. *I am glad you saved her, Mom. I'll be okay.*

Nellie rested her head on top of his. She held him tightly like this until Duncan broke their silence.

And I can never let anyone know? Not Sara...

No. Nellie let go of Duncan. Her words were sharp. *No one can know who, or what, you are. For their safety and for ours.*

Duncan stared at his mother. So he couldn't tell anyone? Duncan could feel pressure of this secret building in his chest.

So, what are we?

Nellie let another sad smile cross her face. *What do you mean, Child?*

You said people thought we were gods, and then other people thought we were demons.

Nellie let her tail rest on his. *We are neither, child. We are what fate has made us, nothing more, nothing less.*

Duncan thought for a moment. *Are the purebreds bad?*

Nellie eyed her son carefully. She had not expected this question. *They are dangerous, yes, but "bad," I cannot say. I suppose in a way they were right. With time, humans and cats did begin to live together in peace once again.* Nellie ran her tail across a dusty bookshelf. She sighed. *But at a cost, we are reliant on humans to feed and care for us, and humans, as they proved long ago, are fickle creatures.*

Duncan shook his head in doubt. *But they sound so mean...*

Nellie laughed dryly. *It's just like in your movies, Duncan. It just depends whose side you're on. After all, do the bad guys in your movies always think they're the "bad guys"?* she asked.

Duncan looked up at his mother, *Well no, they think they're the good guys.*

Exactly the problem, whispered Nellie.

But...

Yes, Duncan?

How could anyone hate us so much? I mean, the way the humans and the other cats hated us?

Nellie stared past her son as she spoke. *Because we're different, Duncan, and all creatures fear those who are different.*

That's it? I mean... we didn't choose this life... it chose us... Duncan's voice trailed off. *It doesn't seem like a reason to hate someone... a reason to kill someone.*

No, it doesn't. Nellie's eyes narrowed. *But one thing I have learned in my life is that as powerful as love is... where love is long dead... hate lives on. And because of that, you and I must stay hidden. We must disappear into the night as Sagira once did.*

The morning was fast approaching, and as they turned to leave, Duncan intentionally brushed his tail across a board game no one knew was there anymore, and because of that no one would ever search for it. Dust particles hovered in the air.

Nellie watched as the specs of dust fell back down into the room of forgotten objects. They clung to her son's coat.

Nellie whispered sadly to herself, *We must gather dust.*

Chapter 5

Duncan pressed his forehead against the cold sliding-glass door. The sun was starting to come up, which meant that very soon his siblings would be awake, and he would no longer be able to sit in silence with his mother watching the sun rise. It also meant that very soon he would have to tell his first of many lies. Can you ever be close to someone without letting them know who you really are? Duncan let his head sink deeper against the glass.

Nellie gently rested her head on his. Her warm breath spread into a thin layer of fog when it hit the cold glass. Duncan could hear his siblings stirring. Nellie turned to tend to them as they began their day. Duncan continued to stare out the window into the rising sun. He watched his mother's breath slowly disappear. Duncan exhaled onto the glass, trying to keep the shape of his mother's breath on the sliding door, but it lingered only for a few seconds and then was gone. He placed his paw into the large imprint left by his mother in the carpet, and for a brief second he felt connected to something sacred and ancient. It was powerful, and it scared him. He wasn't strong enough for this.

Duncan? Duncan felt Sara's tail curl around his.

Hey, Sara.

She leaned against him so that their whiskers touched.

Mom told us that you were sick. Are you feeling any better?

Duncan's eyes narrowed in the growing light. He could hear the concern in her voice.

Sara, unlike Duncan, wasn't watching the sun spread slowly across the grass. She was watching her brother, and the way his eyes looked as he stared out the window made her feel like crying.

A little, he whispered. *What did Mom say about me?*

Sara breathed a sigh of relief. She thought she saw his face relax slightly.

She said you were having a fit, some kind of seizure, and that we needed to let you rest... but you slept so long, I was so worried about you Duncan, I...

Duncan turned to smile reassuringly at his sister.

It's okay, Sara. Duncan patted her tail with his. *I'm better today. See?*

Duncan puffed his tail, stood up on his hind legs, and began to hop from side to side, all while chirping and chattering his teeth. A smile broke across Sara's face. She laughed.

See! I told you, Sara, Duncan chattered.

Duncan had discovered this particular method of cheering his sister up after watching the old cartoon *Rikki Tikki Tavi* with the human family.

The cobras from the movie had scared Sara so much that she had nightmares about snakes coming to kill their family. Whenever she was about to cry, Duncan would do his fighting mongoose impression, and that always seemed to make her smile. She always said he was "*her brave Rikki Tikki*." Duncan only used it in the most serious of circumstances, as Sara was a perpetually cheerful kitten. In the eight weeks of life he had shared with her, she had never gotten upset or angry with him. The only times she had ever cried was when she thought someone in her family was in pain. Duncan smiled at his sister. He wondered if he was really the stronger one.

What do you want to do today, Sis?

Sara was taken aback. She rarely called the shots with her brothers and sisters, and while this suited her just fine, no one had ever asked her what she wanted to do. She savored the moment.

She thought carefully. Duncan didn't rush her.

It was a Wednesday so the human family would be gone for most of the day...

I think... her voice picking up speed to match her excitement. *I think I want to watch "Star Trek"!*

Duncan laughed. *Seriously? Wow, you're such a little nerd.*

Sara grinned. *You're the one who got me hooked on all this stuff!*

All right, all right... Mom! Duncan yelled. *Can you put on Star Trek?*

Use your inside voice, Duncan, and are you sure that won't get you both too worked up?

Nope, Duncan exchanged grins with Sara, who was wriggling with excitement. *It'll have to be Captain Kirk for us today, Mom.*

Nellie eyed her two children the way mothers do when debating whether to give in or to hold their ground. Her eyes softened when they met with Duncan's.

Captain Kirk it is.

~

As Duncan lay on the couch watching spaceships zoom across the television, he couldn't help but think that space seemed a lot lonelier than he remembered. His thoughts were interrupted as he watched his sister stand up on the coffee table and act along with the movie.

"Kahn!!!!!" Sara yelled as she threw her paws up in the air.

Theo nudged Duncan, *She makes a good Shatner.*

~

And so the day went on. After the movie was over, Duncan willingly played any and every game that Sara could think of. They chased mice, crawled up carpet trees, played catch with rainbow balls until Sara could think of nothing more to do but eat her dinner of meaty mush and curl up in a ball with her brothers and sisters in their cardboard bed.

Duncan placed his head on hers until she fell asleep. When he was sure the others had also fallen asleep he carefully stepped out to join his mother as she sat guard.

She's leaving tomorrow.

Yes... it's her time. You didn't say anything to her, did you?

No.

Nellie looked tenderly down at her son. *You are a wonderful brother, Duncan. She'll never forget you.*

I just wish I could tell her goodbye.

Nellie gently nuzzled Duncan's chin with her own. *You did, sweetie, you said it the only way that you could.*

~

That night as Duncan slept, he dreamt of the place from his vision, the strange room that smelled like the young married couple. In his dream he noticed a shadow barely moving on the other side of the closed door. He ran toward it. Maybe it was his mother, maybe it was Sara. *Mom! Sara!* Duncan yelled. *Come back!* He stretched his paw out so that he could reach underneath the door. *Come back!*

He could hear the door opening; maybe he wasn't all alone after all! Duncan recoiled in shock. The vision shattered as his eyes locked with a pair of fuming green eyes.

Duncan awoke with a start.

Kate was shaking his shoulders. *Duncan, wake up, wake up!*

What, what is it, Kate?

It's Sara... Kate's body trembled as she spoke. *She's gone.*

~

The day after Sara left, the kittens said very little to one another. Nellie watched them try to make sense of what had happened as they ate their breakfast in silence. They had never experienced loss before. Watching them eating as they continued to look over at the empty doorway for their lost sister filled her with a mixture of envy and pity. Was it better to be innocent as long as possible, to not yet understand the cruelty of the world you lived in?

She shook her head. It was better to not see what lay ahead of them. That was a burden that, until recently, she had carried alone. Now she shared the weight of it with her son. They would always know what sadness lurked around the corner.

It would happen quickly now. Theo and Emma would be gone soon, and then... she looked back at Duncan, who now was finished with his breakfast and idly batting at a string that hung from the couch. It was one thing to see the future. It was quite another to come to terms with it. She let out a quiet sigh. He needed more training. She would approach him tonight. They had so little time left. Two days. Their eyes met, and she did not need to say a word. He nodded his head. He had seen.

Nellie waited until the other kittens had fallen asleep. She approached their bed and saw that Duncan was waiting for her in the shadow cast by the wall of the box.

He bowed his head so that she could secure her strong jaws around the back of his neck. She leapt deftly over the gate and set Duncan down. He followed silently behind his mother. Tails down, they kept to the shadows.

Nellie turned as they reached the forgotten room. Duncan sat himself down on a tattered, faded box of flash cards. He looked down at a picture of a smiling child pointing and laughing at floating numbers and multiplication signs. He shifted his bottom until the child's face was no longer visible. He did not want an audience tonight.

Nellie tapped her tail on the bookshelf. Duncan watched as the displaced dust floated in and out of a small strip of moonlight.

Yes, Mom?

Do you know why we're meeting tonight, Duncan?

Yes.

Could you tell me please?

You want me to learn how to control my visions... to help me see.

Yes. That is correct, Duncan. Nellie paused.

Your visions will increase in number as you age, but your challenge will be to learn how to make sense of them quickly. We cannot always control when the visions will come, and we cannot always control what the future will allow us to see. There are some things that we cannot see... no matter how hard we try.

Nellie's eyes narrowed slightly.

But Duncan, I brought you here tonight because I wanted you to understand that there is more to your power than just a collection of images. To understand them you have to bring the details of the visions back into the context of your life. You must search your mind and your world to understand their meaning. These images are real, but they will only come to pass depending on the actions you choose to take. Your safety and the safety of those around you depend on your ability to interpret your visions correctly. You must choose when to act, when to watch, and, if necessary, when to run.

Nellie paused, stressing the last few words with grave pride.

We are Children of Sagira, Duncan. We possess the gift of sight, and though it may at times seem like the gift possesses us... please try to see it as a gift... remember to treat it as such.

Nellie stopped.

Do you understand?

Yes, Mom.

Then we shall begin. What was your last vision, Duncan?

Duncan hesitated, remembering the angry green eyes. He lied.

I saw Theo & Emma leave.

Okay, Duncan, said Nellie softly, examining her son's taut face. He was hiding something from her. *Describe to me what you saw.*

~

And so the night moved forward. Duncan describing what he saw and Nellie pushing him to draw details from the images.

Stretch your mind. What time did the clock say?

7... 7:30, I think.

Whose eyes were you seeing through?

Mine, I think.

Are you sure?

No, no wait, I can see myself. I'm sleeping. We all are. They're picking Theo up, now Emma... Duncan closed his eyes. Oddly enough, he could see better that way.

Nellie whispered in his ear. *Leave your body behind... whose eyes are you seeing through?*

Her voice was hypnotic. Duncan let himself sink into the vision. It was the same sensation he'd felt standing by the sliding-glass door while he watched the sun rise. His stomach felt heavy, like he might throw up. His head was spinning. It all still felt too big for him. Whose eyes was he looking through? He could feel the air from an open window. He looked down. He saw his mother's feet.

Your eyes! They're your eyes.

Good, Duncan. She gave her son a tired smile.

Question after question followed until Duncan could see the answers before him almost instantly as Nellie asked the questions.

Can you tell when this will happen, Duncan?

Duncan opened his eyes. Strange how what he had seen had been so much clearer than what surrounded him right now.

In just a few hours. This morning, while we're asleep.

Nellie let out a deep sigh. The patch of moonlight had begun to shift from silver to gold. Morning was approaching. *It is time for us to go. Tomorrow night I will teach you how to blind others with your visions. It is a skill to be used only if you have no other choice. It is our best defense against those who would hurt us, as well as our best protection for those who are closest to us. It is how we stay hidden.*

Nellie turned and began to glide back through the shadows.

Come quickly Duncan, we must get you back before they come for Theo and Emma.

Mom?

Yes, Duncan, walk and talk, dear.

Mom?

Will you and I always see the same visions?

No, Duncan. Nellie picked up her pace. *Only for as long as our lives are intertwined. That was why you could see through my eyes. Once our paths change, so do our visions.*

Oh, said Duncan sadly.

You may find that you see through someone else's eyes in your life after me.

Duncan was about ask his mother what she meant when she raised her paw to silence him.

Nellie slowed a few steps back from the makeshift kitten gate. Her mind flashed to the night Duncan was born. Her selfishness had doomed him to this life, all because she thought for one brief moment that she was safe, that she was in control of her future. Her love for Duncan's father had caused her to take chances. She gazed into her son's face. His father had left her and soon Duncan would do the same. She would not let Duncan make her mistakes. They were Children of Sagira, and they must walk alone.

Nellie moved her face close to her son's. Her eyes focused on him with such intensity that Duncan felt a shiver run down his spine. Her whisper was almost a hiss.

Duncan, never assume you are safe just because you have not had a vision warning you of danger. Just because we can see the future doesn't mean we are in control of that future. We may choose to guide it, yes, but we will never control it. You will never... Nellie started again, her voice straining. *Because of what you are, you will never be safe. You must never let your guard down. If you do, you will only hurt the ones you love.*

Do you understand?

Duncan was startled by the sudden urgency in his mother's voice. He nodded and whispered back because they were getting close now. *We walk alone.*

Nellie moved toward the gate and Duncan extended his neck for her to grab. He does not understand, not yet, she thought to herself. Nellie landed softly on her paws on the other side of the gate. She set him down and whispered softly in his ear so as not to wake his siblings.

Tomorrow night will be your final lesson.

Chapter 6

Duncan lay quietly watching his siblings sleep. When he woke up, Theo and Emma would be gone. He buried himself farther into their flannel blanket. Tonight was different from his last night with Sara, but Theo was his brother and Emma his sister, and the thought of losing them too made him feel like someone was clawing at his insides. At least they will have each other, Duncan thought to himself. He turned so that he could see them both and reluctantly closed his eyes.

While he slept, Duncan once again dreamed of the angry green-eyed cat.

Who was she? It was a she, he was sure of it. And why did she stare at him with such hatred? He had never met her before. How could she hate someone she didn't even know? Duncan felt himself clenching his jaw in his sleep, grinding his teeth against one another, but he could not stop the dream. *Who are you?* He kept asking the mysterious cat. Each time he got close she would hiss, flash a set of tiny white fangs, and then dart off into the darkness. Each time he would be picked up by the young married woman and placed back in the room... always on the wrong side of the door. *Let me out!* Duncan cried. *Who are you? Why won't you speak to me? My name is Duncan! My name is Duncan!* He pounded his paws against the door.

Duncan. It was Kate tapping him on the shoulder. *I think you were having a nightmare. You kept crying out in your sleep.*

Oh, Duncan shook his head groggily. *What did I say?*

Kate shifted her gaze uncomfortably. *A lot of stuff, nothing I could really make out.*

Duncan breathed a sigh of relief. *Where are Theo and Emma?* It was late, they must have been gone by now. He hated lying to his siblings.

Kate's black whiskers drooped, *They're gone, just like Sara.* She stared off in the direction of the doorway. *They must be taking us while we're asleep.*

Duncan lifted his head to look at Kate. She was a beautiful kitten. She had long, brown tabby fur, just like Emma's. And just as his eyes were slowly turning yellow, he could see that her blue eyes were now turning green. Duncan sighed. Kate had no idea that she and Anna would be the ones staying with their mother. She would never have to leave. He had seen it. Duncan felt a surge of jealously rush through his body. They didn't need their mother the way he did. They had nothing to hide.

Kate was still staring at him. He turned his eyes away, feeling guilty. It wasn't their fault, he reminded himself. Their paths were set.

He rose stiffly to go to the litter box. Nighttime training sessions made for exhausting days. He yawned and rubbed at his eyes with his paw as he entered the dome. Kate followed quickly behind him.

Uh, Sis? Little privacy? Duncan pawed at the litter awkwardly.

Oh, right! Sorry! Kate turned around but refused to leave.

It's just... I miss Theo and Emma. Today we were going to reenact the Battle of the Alamo.

Duncan smiled. It was obvious what special had been on the History Channel this week.

Duncan pawed through the litter, making a neat little pile in the corner. *Sorry, Sis, I don't know anything about the Battle of the Alamo.*

Well then, what are we going to do today?

Where's Anna?

She said that if you came up with something fun to do then she'd play with us, otherwise she'd rather climb the curtains or shred the lampshades.

Duncan looked longingly back at their bed.

Well? asked Kate.

It appeared that with Theo gone, Duncan was now in charge of playtime activities. This was rather unfortunate as he was hoping to spend the day sleeping, but one look at Kate with both paws sunk into the litter made him realize that she wasn't budging until he came up with something entertaining that involved her.

Can we talk about this somewhere else? asked Duncan.

Kate stared blankly back at him.

Duncan lowered his voice. *Somewhere where we're not surrounded by poo?*

Kate wrinkled her nose. *Fair enough, but do you promise to play with us?*

Yeah, yeah, I promise, grumbled Duncan, with the irritated tone of a brother being nagged by his sister.

Once they exited, Kate began to trot alongside Duncan. Her stride was shorter than his, and it took a considerable effort on her part to keep up with him.

Well? What's your plan?

My plan?

Yes, Theo always had a plan.

Duncan frowned. *Hmm, well, I don't know much about history, but...*

Yes, yes, go on...

I guess I do know a lot about spaceships and robots and stuff. We could have a space battle?

Kate paused to evaluate her brother's offer. Apparently, being faced with a day of extreme boredom, filled only with thoughts of her lost siblings, had made Kate more willing to join Duncan in one of his space adventures.

For instance, Duncan called down as he climbed up their scratching post, *this can be our Battlestar!* He used his body weight to tip the post forward onto the ground.

Go grab Anna, and we'll play.

Kate took a long look at her brother, who was now straddling his carpeted spaceship, shrugged, and ran off to find her sister.

Duncan laughed for the first time in the last several days. The humans had left the fan on and it was blowing in his fur. It was nice to escape, even only for a little while.

Kate returned, followed by their very reluctant sister.

Come on, Anna, Kate nudged, *it'll be fun*

Are you sure about that? replied Anna skeptically.

Duncan hopped down from his ship and wrapped his tail around Anna's shoulders.

Come on Anna, I'll let you use a phaser!

A what?

Duncan's mouth fell open. He was stunned. *They're only the coolest weapon ever! "Set your phaser to kill"? Oh, come on, don't you watch any TV?*

Anna still looked unconvinced, *You know I don't watch your sci-fi shows.*

Duncan added, *You get to shoot things...*

Anna's ears perked up.

Duncan continued, *Yeah, you and Kate will take over the ship by posing as loyal crew members, and then, when I least expect it, you'll attack!*

Like a mutiny? Kate cried excitedly.

Duncan and Anna both stared in surprise at their normally nonviolent sister.

What? I saw it when the humans watched that pirate movie downstairs. The pirates mutinied. I liked it.

Duncan laughed. Even Anna was smiling. *No, Kate, that's really good, yeah, you'll mutiny.*

Kate clapped her paws together.

So, you guys in?

Let me get this straight... Anna eyed her brother suspiciously... *I get to take over your ship? By force? With a phaser thingy?*

Duncan nodded.

Fine, I'm in.

~

The day passed quickly. Before they knew it, it was time for dinner, a quick tongue bath, and then bedtime. Even though Anna, Kate, and Duncan were rapidly outgrowing their cardboard bed, Duncan thought it felt empty with just the three of them.

Stretching his body so that his back paws hung off the edge of the cardboard, Duncan lay waiting for the night to come. He would never admit it, but he was nervous. He was just now getting used to having the visions. Thankfully his body no longer went rigid or seized. All that preceded and followed his visions was the sensation of pressure building behind his eyes. It wasn't an enjoyable feeling, but more importantly, it was something he could hide. Nellie had reassured him that to anyone watching, it would look like he was drifting in and out of a very light sleep.

Duncan stretched his forearm so that it covered his eyes. He had been having more visions of the young married couple and of their mysterious green-eyed cat, but strangely enough, he had not had any of leaving his family (at least not since the young couple's last visit). But he knew it was coming soon. He could feel it. But when? Surely his mom would say something if she knew? She'd want to say goodbye, wouldn't she?

Duncan paused. He remembered all too clearly the day she blinded him, what it felt like, the color of her eyes when they flashed. He felt his paws tremble involuntarily from the power of the memory.

He wondered what it'd feel like to do that to someone... if he even could do it. He inhaled deeply. *Only one more lesson left*, he whispered. He turned to look at his sisters. They were sound asleep. Their soft bellies rose and fell in unison, and their whiskers and paws twitched as they dreamt of normal kitten things, like birds and mice and meaty mush. Duncan watched them sadly. His dreams were no longer like theirs, he thought to himself. His were real, and there was no waking up.

Duncan quietly exited the bed and dropped his head to allow his mother to grab his neck, but as he lowered his eyes, he noticed that the humans had removed their makeshift gate.

They must be preparing for when I'm gone.

But before the weight of this thought had time to sink in, Nellie gestured for him to follow her.

~

Duncan took his usual place in the forgotten room, and Nellie moved alongside him. Duncan couldn't quite place it, but something was different about his mother tonight. She kept looking at the doorway.

53

And then, just like flipping a switch, Nellie was calm. Eyeing the clock, she turned to face him.

Tonight is the most important lesson I will ever teach you, Duncan. I tell you this not to scare you, but I want you to know that this aspect of our gift was what made us the most feared of Sagira's Children. To burn, to become invisible, to persuade... it is nothing compared to being able to take another person's eyes from them. There may come a day when you will have to blind another so that you may continue to see.

Duncan nodded, his eyes wide and unblinking.

Nellie continued. *Do you remember the day I blinded you? How strong the effect was?*

Duncan nodded. He dug his claws into the carpet to steady himself.

Its effect on you was nothing compared to the effect it would have on someone who was not one of us.

Duncan's ears fell back. *But... I slept for hours!*

Yes, and someone who is not one of us will sleep on and off for days. They will not remember what happened to them, and if you are not careful, your attack could kill them, or perhaps worse, drive them mad.

Duncan stared at his mother in disbelief.

Their minds are not meant to see the things we see. Nellie took another step forward. *That is why you must listen and memorize everything I teach you tonight. You must blind anyone who is a danger to you. Can you do that for me, Duncan?*

Nellie softened when she saw the fear in her son's eyes.

Yes, Mom, replied Duncan, *I can do that.*

Then we shall begin. Duncan, I need you to raise your eyes so that they are within a few inches of mine. The closer you are, the more powerful your attack.

Duncan did as he was told.

Now, I want you to concentrate on a vision you've had. Re-create it in your mind.

Nellie waited for a few minutes while Duncan sat, deep in concentration, his dark brow furrowed and his eyes were clamped tightly shut.

Do you have it?

Duncan did. He could see two perfect, fierce green eyes staring back at him. She was sitting on a window ledge. Though she was small, she cast a large shadow. Her tail was bobbed, and it twitched with disgust as she stared down at him.

Now this is the tricky part. You must channel the vision, let it become the only part of you that moves.

Moves?

Slow your mind, slow your body, make everything around you stand still. Breathe into the vision. Free it. At the core of each vision there is a power, a flame that wants to be unleashed. You've felt it before, Duncan. There is ancient power inside you. Set it free.

Duncan could feel a heat building inside of him, and the pressure behind his eyes was almost unbearable.

Now open your eyes

Mom? I don't think I can control it.

Open your eyes, Duncan. Trust me.

Duncan's eyes flashed a dark gold. They reflected back in his mother's pupils.

Nellie searched her son's face. So this was what he had been keeping from her. She paused, thinking of the green-eyed cat and wondering what else her son had seen. The fur on her back rose slightly. After tonight, she would not be able to protect him.

Duncan raised a paw and gently touched his mother's face, *Did I hurt you?*

Nellie smiled weakly, drawn back into the present by her son's touch. *No, dear.*

Duncan cocked his head to the side.

Are you disappointed? asked Nellie.

No, said Duncan sheepishly. *I just don't want to hurt you.*

Well, we will keep practicing until you do. Now try again.

But... I don't want...

Do not be afraid, Duncan. I am strong enough for this. You must learn how to defend yourself. Now, try again.

Flash.

Again.

Flash.

Good, again.

Flash.

They practiced blinding until Duncan managed to make Nellie buckle slightly at the knees.

Good, Duncan, Nellie whispered in a tired voice. *Very good.*

Mom? Duncan? asked a small voice echoing in the doorway.

Duncan wheeled around.

Anna? What are you doing here?

I woke up. I didn't want them to take me. Her eyes began to well up with tears, *So I went looking for you, and I saw...*

Duncan turned to his mother.

I'm sorry, Duncan.

Looking from his mother to Anna, he realized what his mother intended to do. *No, you can't! She's not strong enough, you said it yourself!* cried Duncan.

There are times you have to make a choice, Duncan, she whispered.

Duncan looked back at Anna. She was trembling. No, how could his mother do this?

Duncan ran in front of his sister.

I won't let you, Duncan yelled.

I'm sorry, Duncan, repeated Nellie, more urgently this time. *I have no choice.*

Duncan's whole body was shaking. *You're our mother!*

Anna's eyes rolled back into her head, her knees buckled, and she fell to the floor.

No! cried Duncan as he rushed to his sister's side.

Duncan, spoke Nellie softly, *I need you to look at me.*

No, no... Mom, not like this!

Nellie raised his chin with her paw. *This is the price we paid to save her life. We must continue to pay it.*

Duncan, I love you. Be strong. She smiled sadly, and flashed her golden eyes.

Duncan saw an image of his mother resting her head gently on his as they watched the sun rise... and then she was gone.

~

Duncan felt himself struggling against the darkness. He could see his body being lifted up from their cardboard bed. Anna and Kate lay sleeping. The young married couple stood over them smiling; the rosy-faced woman held him in her arms and gently placed him into a small crate. "Little guy really is out"... she whispered. If she only knew that he wouldn't, he couldn't wake. The couple crowded their heads in front of the crate. He could no longer see himself. The vision flashed, and he was suddenly watching from an upstairs window. He could see the crate carrying his unconscious body as it was placed into a small red vehicle. He saw the pattern of familiar breath forming on the window. The car slowly began to pull away. He watched as a paw reached up and pressed itself against the basement window. He knew the shape of it well. It would never clean, scold, or comfort him again. He could hear her voice. *To be special is to be different, and to be different is to be alone.* As the car turned around the corner, he felt the vision begin to slip away from him.

We will share visions only as long as our lives are intertwined, his mother had told him. *Once our paths change, so do our visions.*

It was time for Duncan-Son of Nellie, Child of Sagira-to walk alone.

PART TWO

Chapter 7

Duncan woke with a splitting headache. He was in the room from his visions, only it was dark. Based on when they had taken him, it must still be early morning. They must have decided to let him sleep. Duncan raised his head to examine his surroundings. He had been sleeping in a small plastic carrier with a metal door propped open.

His mouth felt dry. Water, he needed water.

Where had he seen it? Duncan rubbed his paws over his bleary eyes. There, they were exactly where they had been in his visions. Duncan walked stiffly over to two small bowls, one filled with water, the other with meaty mush. He drank deeply. His stomach clenched. No food, not yet. He could see his reflection in the water bowl. There was no more blue left in his eyes, only bright gold. Duncan dipped his paw in the water to disrupt the floating image.

Though he had seen this place many times, it still didn't feel real. He began to groom himself vigorously. He felt dirty, out of sorts. Angrily, he kicked over the bowl of water and watched as the liquid soaked into the cream carpet. Exhausted, he turned back toward the carrier, pressed his body against the cold plastic, and waited for his new life to begin.

~

Several hours later, the married couple entered the room. Duncan raised his head. Ignoring them, he stumbled to his litter box. He sneezed. Eesh, this stuff smelled far too fresh. Well, he'd fix that soon enough. This was an open top litter box, and it was certainly different from what he had been using. Duncan frowned. It was no space ship.

After he had finished and climbed out, the young woman smothered him with kisses and what sounded like garbled words of praise. It was high pitched and filled with lots of cooing noises. Good grief, you'd think he'd accomplished something extraordinary. Duncan sighed. It was going to take very little to impress this woman.

While he wasn't in the mood to play, Duncan decided to allow the woman to rub behind his ears and under his chin. What reason did he have to get out of bed anymore? There were no more training sessions to wait for, just a life filled with praise for peeing in a sandbox.

The young man left and returned with fresh meaty mush and a new bowl of water. He set it down on a towel.

As he approached the food bowl, Duncan heard the faint clicking of claws outside the door. He had nearly forgotten, the green-eyed cat! He ran to the door and the man cracked it open to reveal two furious little eyes. He knew them well.

She hissed.

Duncan smiled. He'd seen this so many times.

Confused by his reaction, she puffed her fur larger and hissed again.

Hi, my name is Duncan. What's y--?

Ears back, she glared at Duncan. Arching her neck, the girl cat uttered a low growl and raised her small white paw. Stopping just inches from his face, she made sure Duncan could see each of her well-sharpened claws. In one swift motion she turned and ran back into the hall.

The man shut the door and turned to the woman. "This is going to take a while." The woman looked as if she was going to burst into tears. "Why don't they like each other?" she started to cry into her husband's shoulder.

Duncan listened to the woman weep as he grabbed a mouthful of mush and chewed. Perhaps this place was going to be more interesting than he'd thought.

~

The humans spent the rest of the day attempting to introduce Duncan to the green-eyed cat. The woman kept referencing a large book with a picture of a kitten on it.

"It says to use food!"

"I know it says that, but she won't eat it. I've tried."

"I'm out of ideas!"

"Well, let's go back to Chapter One and try again"

The woman sighed and picked Duncan up. "Here we go, my little Dunkelberry"...

Duncan rolled his eyes, Dunkelberry, of all the nicknames...

The man opened the door leading out of the familiar room. The small black-and-white cat sat on a bookshelf in the hallway. Her tail stub rotated in angry circles.

Duncan found himself being turned around back-end first in front of the nameless girl cat.

Duncan couldn't see her face, but he tried to wave his tail in a friendly hello. *Hi, my name is Duncan.*

The girl cat's nose twitched in disgust. Still nothing. The woman moved his back-end closer to the girl cat. She hissed.

Suddenly very self-conscious, Duncan tried again. It can't be that bad. He was sure he had washed this morning. *My name is Duncan, What's your name?* Still nothing.

The woman moved Duncan even closer to the black-and-white cat's face. Duncan could hear the sounds of hissing and growling dangerously near his rear.

Duncan struggled nervously. He wasn't sure how much longer he wanted to have his back-end on display to such a hostile audience.

The woman sighed and turned Duncan so that he was facing forward. "Well, I guess we'll just keep trying until she comes around."

Duncan groaned. He could see the girl cat's eyes widen. The thought of repeated butt-sniffing introductions didn't sit well with her either.

"Look, honey! She's finally coming around! Set him down!"

Purring! Yes, the little black-and-white cat was purring!

Duncan found himself face to face with the pair of eyes he had once feared. Perhaps his initial reaction was the correct one.

Hi... ummm... my name is Duncan. What's your name?

Duncan took a long look at her face. She was much smaller than his mother but older. He could see traces of white speckled throughout her black fur. Her feet were booted white, and she had long ivory whiskers that framed her mouth and accented her large green eyes. She had a white ruff and a small white patch on her muzzle. When she opened her mouth he could see that many of her teeth were missing. She leaned forward and whispered in his ear.

I had no intention of ever speaking to you, but I'll drown myself in my own water bowl if I have to sit here and sniff your butt for the rest of my afternoon. And just so we're clear, this is my house. These are my people. Do not touch me. Do not touch any of my things. Do not talk to me. Do not get in my way, or I will make you very... very... sorry. She dug her claws into the hardwood. *Understand, Dunkelberry?*

Duncan's ears fell back in shock.

Good. The girl cat smiled and trotted off down the hall. Over her shoulder she whispered, *Enjoy your stay... however long you last.*

As Duncan continued to sit in stunned disbelief, the young woman hugged her husband.

"They're going to be such wonderful friends!"

Chapter 8

Duncan watched as the girl cat disappeared around the corner.

His visions had not prepared him for any of this.

Duncan followed tentatively down the hallway after the humans. It appeared that he had free rein over the house. This would have been an exciting moment for him had he not just been threatened by a miniature black-and-white she-cougar.

Pull yourself together, Duncan! This is your house now too, he muttered to himself. Duncan tried to walk more confidently as he examined his new home. Let's see... three bedrooms, one-and-a-half baths... not bad. The house was smaller than the one he had shared with his mother and his brother and sisters, but it had a warm and cozy feel to it, not including the hostile intentions of the girl cat.

Duncan stepped out of the hallway into a larger room. This was the path that the girl cat had taken, and he had chosen it as the last room to explore for precisely that reason. With a deep breath Duncan trotted quickly into the room. It was overflowing with electronics, and in the center... the largest television Duncan had ever seen. It was beautiful. With some effort Duncan tore his eyes from the television to scan for the girl cat.

She was sitting perched on the edge of a large maroon couch. She glared down at Duncan, grunted, sat up, and turned so that she was no longer facing him.

Duncan tentatively hopped up onto the couch. The girl cat raised her head sharply. Duncan didn't need to see her face to know that the couch was on the list of things that he was never to touch. He quickly jumped down to the floor. The girl cat slowly lowered her head back down.

Duncan exhaled with disappointment. He looked around the room. In the corner sat an old wooden chair with two curved legs on the bottom. As Duncan tried to pull himself up the chair, it rocked violently forward, throwing him backward onto the floor. He landed with a small thud. Great, thought Duncan, just great.

He could hear purring from the couch. Fine, he grumbled. Carpet is better anyway.

Duncan stretched himself out. He spent most of his day watching the television with the humans. Every now and then one of them would stop to throw a stuffed mouse or rainbow ball for him. Each time he brought the toy back. He wanted to make a good impression. He thought he could see the girl cat roll her eyes at him, but then again, it was difficult for him distinguish between her varied looks of contempt. As he watched her, he found himself wondering if it was his presence that caused her to look so perpetually angry. It was hard to ever imagine her face with anything but a scowl draped across it.

69

So the day went on, Duncan keeping his distance, the girl cat sitting crossly on her couch, and the humans remaining blissfully ignorant.

During meal-time, Duncan waited patiently while the girl cat ate. At one point Duncan thought about asking whether or not she'd realized she was eating all the meaty mush, but thought better of it as he watched her remaining teeth break down the kibble that lay underneath. When it came his turn to eat, Duncan found the meaty mush had been licked clean off so that only the half-eaten kibble remained. *Lovely*, he grumbled to himself.

When it came time for bed, Duncan curled up on the very edge of the human bed by the man's feet. He was surprised at first that the girl cat allowed this until he realized how often the man's feet kicked throughout the night.

While this was annoying in its own right, the man's feet weren't the reason for Duncan's inability to sleep. As the woman was getting ready for bed, Duncan had heard her confirm his fears. Tomorrow was Monday. And just like his previous humans, this meant that the young married couple was going to work, and he was going to spend the whole day with the cat who was currently polishing her claws on the other side of bed.

During what fitful sleep he did get, Duncan had a vision of himself curled up next to the girl cat. She had her head placed tenderly on his stomach. They looked... like friends.

Duncan awoke just in time to avoid the sweeping motion of a large foot flopping across the bed. The girl cat was sleeping on the human woman's pillow, with one green eye left open, filled with suspicion and disgust, and it was fixed directly on him. Yeah right, muttered Duncan, shaking off the warmth of the vision, we're going to be the best of friends...

~

Duncan could hear the humans stirring. He kept his eyes shut. Maybe if he refused to get out of bed, the day would never start. He burrowed his head under his paws.

Oh! But he could hear the sounds of the fridge opening, bowls being set on the counter, a fresh can of meaty mush popping open! Duncan's stomach rumbled.

It was too tempting. Duncan carefully made his way out into the kitchen. The girl cat was already there, sitting primly on the tile, paws together, and purring loudly at the woman.

While they waited, Duncan lowered his head to get a drink of water. He was shocked at his reflection. His fur was a mess! Since he'd left home he'd spent less time grooming, but wow, if his mother could see him now, he'd get such a licking. A pang of sadness ran through him, a reminder that he was on his own. He looked at himself again in the water. His fur was flattened on the left side and sticking out every which way on the right. He dipped his paw in the water bowl, gave it a good lick and attempted to straighten out his fur. He gave up as soon as the bowl of meaty mush hit the ground.

Duncan felt his fear turn to excitement. Once the humans were gone he didn't have to play by the rules. Duncan ate his breakfast with renewed spirit. He was a Child of Sagira. Who cared if the girl cat was bigger than he was? He was faster and stronger. Nine weeks old and growing, he would soon be a tomcat. He should act like one. The girl cat bumped him away from his food. Duncan felt a smile spread across his face for the first time since he had left his home. This cat had no idea who she was dealing with.

~

The girl cat watched as the humans closed the door.

She stretched herself out on the couch and pressed the red power button on the remote.

Duncan hopped up beside her. *Ooh, what are we watching?*

Glare.

"Days of Our Lives"? Can't we watch something else? Duncan reached for the remote.

Hiss. The girl cat slapped his paw. She wiped it on the couch and wrinkled her nose as though she had touched something repulsive and filthy.

Fine, fine, we'll watch your soap operas. Duncan rolled his eyes. What a middle-aged house cat. *This looks boring.*

Glare. The girl cat was clearly annoyed. She hit the volume button up.

Duncan smiled. If he had learned anything from being a brother, it was how to be truly, deeply annoying. *Why do you think they talk out loud to themselves?*

Volume 56.

Are those two related? They look related. Then why are they kissing?

Volume 59.

Do you ever wonder why there are never any cats on these shows?

Volume 61.

Why is that woman watching from the bushes? She's not very well hidden. You'd think they'd see her... and there she goes talking to herself again! Shhh, don't make noise, they'll find you!

Volume 75.

How many people do you think are really named Dakota?

TV off!

Oh, good! Do you want to talk now? I still don't know your name. The humans call you, Sweetie. Would you like me to call you, Sweetie?

A set of claws flew past Duncan's nose as he quickly ducked out of the way.

That wasn't very nice.

I told you to leave me alone! She hissed. The small cat glared. Her green eyes were slits in the daylight. She took a deep breath and exhaled forcefully through her nose. Duncan thought she looked like a minature bull ready to charge.

To his surprise, she turned and walked off into the kitchen and leapt onto a very high windowsill. She smiled down at Duncan. She knew he couldn't jump that high yet. She tucked all four paws under her black-and-white patched stomach.

Ooo, you're going to nap in the sun? Mind if I join?

Duncan began finding footholds in the human's wine rack. *Let's see, wait, wait, I got it!* Duncan pulled himself up as the wine bottles rattled violently. The girl cat's eyes widened.

Duncan thought to himself, *Yes, that's right, little Miss "this is my house." This is your life now.*

~

Duncan spent the next three days harassing the girl cat in an effort to get her to tell him her name. He sang annoying songs that he made up as he went along. When he got bored with that, he recited movies. Not short children's movies either. No, Duncan insisted on epic trilogies.

Judge me by my tail size, do you?

Let the force flow through you, young Catwalker.

He restaged light saber fights using his tail, complete with sound effects and running leaps off the couch.

On and on, Duncan acted out famous scenes from his favorite movies while the girl cat tried to block out Duncan's relentless voice. She even tried to plug her ears with plush mice, but after deciding that they weren't effective, she gave up and watched the little fool pretend to lose his paw in a light saber battle.

There was nowhere the girl cat could go that Duncan wouldn't follow.

Duncan used every tactic he had for harassing someone into talking to him, but so far the girl cat held strong. Duncan had even tried to use his power to see if he could figure out her name through a vision, but so much of the girl cat was hidden from him. He did, however, have an uncanny knack for seeing what the humans were going to pack in their lunches. He knew when to be by the fridge for deli meat scraps and when to sleep in on days that they packed peanut butter. However, it wasn't until their sixth day together that Duncan finally learned the name of the girl cat, and it wasn't through a vision.

He had spent the previous five days studying the girl cat. Each morning she ate her breakfast, took a 10-minute bath, watched her soap operas, took a litter box break, took another bath, ate a light lunch of kibble, and then found a spot to nap where the sun hit the western-facing windows. She stayed sleeping until the humans returned in the evening.

In an attempt to break her down, Duncan had taken to banging on the blinds during her afternoon naps. He'd heard Theo talk about how sleep deprivation could make prisoners talk, and Duncan was determined to get this little middle-aged house cat to sing.

After five days alone with Duncan, it appeared the girl cat was reaching her breaking point.

Will you, through clenched teeth she hissed the next words, *please... shut up!*

Duncan smiled. *But I'm just dusting the blinds.*

They don't need dusting. They're fine. You're fine. I'm the only one in this forsaken place who's not fine!

Duncan played dumb. *Why aren't you fine?*

The girl cat yowled, *BECAUSE YOU WON'T SHUT YOUR KIBBLE HOLE!*

Well, I guess I could be quiet, but...

But what? She spit out the words.

I really wish you'd tell me your name.

75

Silence.

But I guess, Duncan raised his paw to the blinds.

The girl cat sighed deeply and jumped down from her windowsill.

Fine. My name is Wh--

Duncan's eyes began to flutter. No! Not now!

This vision was strong. His knees felt weak. Everything was getting darker, and then...

Red, gold, fire! Consuming everything!

Duncan awoke to the girl cat fanning him with her stub of a tail.

I think, I think I'm going to be....

Duncan vomited his lunch onto the cherry-wood floor.

Sick? The girl cat asked sarcastically.

Duncan's paws trembled. What was happening to him? Oh no, the darkness was coming back.

He could feel her dragging him by the scruff of the neck.

Lord, you're fat.

Duncan's stomach lurched.

Fine, fine, you're just big-boned. Just don't yack all over the floor again.

Where was she taking him?

On no, she was going to kill him! She knew! She knew who he was!

This was it.

Just, Duncan gagged, he was overcome by nausea and heat. *Just tell me your name before you kill me.*

Duncan thought he heard laughter. She was more twisted than he thought.

He felt himself land on something soft.

What?

The girl cat's whiskers were curled with amusement.

Duncan's eyes were closing. He wouldn't be conscious much longer.

My name is Whiski, and I don't plan on killing you.

He could hear her laughter fading away. *At least not until after I've had my nap.*

Chapter 9

Duncan opened his eyes slowly and with great effort. They felt heavy, like they had been welded shut by the heat of the vision.

What had he seen? And why had it affected him so much? Duncan let his eyelids close. They still felt hot. He tried to pull back the vision, but all he could see was fire. He needed water. Dragging himself to the kitchen, Duncan dipped his paw in the water bowl and washed his face. Even his saliva was hot. He was still nauseous from before, but at least his secret was safe. The girl cat didn't know. Duncan looked out the bedroom window. He had kept his promise to his mother.

The sun was setting. The humans would be home soon. Where was the girl cat? Where was Whiski?

Duncan scanned the room. Hah! Still sleeping.

Whiski lay curled in a ball in a fading strip of sunlight. Her feet and whiskers were twitching. She was dreaming.

Duncan wondered if he should wake her.

Stop! She murmured and batted at the air.

A smile spread across Duncan's face. She was dreaming of him no doubt. *I wonder what I'm up to,* he chuckled to himself. He rather enjoyed the idea of a dream-Duncan tormenting a dream-Whiski.

No, please, stop! No! Her paws began to flail wildly against the couch cushions. *I'll do anything! Please, stop!*

Duncan stopped smiling. His shoulders sank. Whiski was whimpering in her sleep. Whatever was tormenting her, he'd never seen anyone look so small and terrified. He had to wake her. Duncan lifted his still-aching body onto the couch and moved cautiously toward the girl cat.

Whiski? Duncan brushed his tail across her shoulders. *Whiski?*

Her eyes snapped open and her remaining teeth locked around his tail. In the midst of his pain, Duncan made a mental note that she still had all four fangs. He could feel each one as they threatened to puncture his skin.

Gah! Ouch! Duncan yowled.

Whiski's green eyes changed from being filled with fear to being filled with anger. She released her jaws. *What are you doing? I told you not to touch me!*

I... Duncan stopped. *Are you okay?*

Whiski averted her eyes and began grooming herself defensively.

Duncan took a step back. *You were dreaming.*

Whiski turned so that her back was to him. *So? Everyone dreams.*

Not like that, replied Duncan softly. He raised his paw in concern. *What happened to you? Who was hurting you?*

Whiski growled. *What? You think we're friends now?* She was almost spitting she was so furious. *Just because I helped you today doesn't change anything! I don't know you! I don't want to know you!* Whiski head-butted Duncan backward so that he lost his balance and tumbled off the couch. *You're just a stupid little kitten who thinks he can do whatever he wants and nothing bad will ever happen to him. You don't know the first thing about life, and you don't know the first thing about me!* Her shoulders were hunched, and her chest was rising and falling rapidly.

Duncan began slowly backing up. *I'm sorry, I... just... I'm sorry.* He swallowed hard. He didn't know what else to say.

Just do yourself a favor and stay away from me! Whiski looked down at Duncan. Her green eyes were filled with pain as she growled. *Some cats are meant to live alone.*

Duncan tried, but he couldn't look her in the eyes. Instead, he nodded, keeping his ancient yellow eyes fixed on the ground.

~

The humans were finishing their bedtime routine. Whiski let her claws sink deep into her scratching post. She'd hurt his feelings. She let out an exasperated sigh. Duncan was just a kid, an annoying one, but then again, all kittens were annoying. Whiski rolled her eyes thinking of all the foster kittens she'd had to live with before she'd found her nice quiet home with the human couple. She shook her head, trying to rid herself of the nagging feeling of guilt that had been trailing her all evening. The truth was that he didn't deserve the verbal slap in the face, and the very nonverbal bite to the tail, that she'd given him. He was just trying to be nice.

Whiski dug deeper into the scratching post. What was wrong with her? She didn't need nice. She needed to be left alone, far away from any, and all, preteen boy cats.

The night with the humans had passed without either cat speaking a word. When the time came to go to sleep, Duncan had still not attempted to approach her, much less talk to her.

Why did this bother her? She'd spent the last week trying to get him to shut up, and now that he had, well, she found herself feeling guilty.

Whiski let her stump of a tail tap in frustration against the comforter. While she'd lost most of her tail when she was a kitten, she often felt as though she could still feel it flicking and curling in the air along with her moods. She hadn't experienced feelings like this in a very long time. She looked over at Duncan lying on the human's dresser by the window. She could already tell by the size of his paws that he was going to be a large cat. She had to thoroughly intimidate him now. Whiski looked down at her white paws. Her mother had called her *dainty... a delicate feline.* Whiski hated it. Dainty, delicate, those just sounded like pretty ways to describe a cat who needed to be taken care of, a cat who needed someone else to save her. Whiski grimaced. She'd known at an early age that she wouldn't be satisfied sitting on the sidelines. By 10 weeks she'd been able to pin her brother, who was easily twice her size. *A lady doesn't fight like that,* her mother used to say. *Good thing I'm not a lady,* she'd always growl back.

Whiski stared wistfully out the window. She missed her brother. He had been her companion for the first five years of her life. He had never made fun of her for being small or for having a stump for a tail. He was kind and strong and he knew how to make her feel like everything was going to be okay, even when she knew better. But he was gone now, and ever since, Whiski thought he'd taken the best part of her with him. That was three years ago, before the shelters, before the kind young couple, and long before Duncan.

Duncan was watching the sunrise from the bedroom window. He pressed his head to the glass and watched sadly as his breath formed patterns against the giant windowpane. Whiski's heart sank. He reminded her of her brother. That was the problem.

Whiski inhaled deeply and rolled her eyes thinking over what she was about to do. The humans were already snoring soundly as she stepped over them.

Hey, kid.

Duncan cocked his ears back slightly, but otherwise gave no acknowledgement of her presence.

Whiski sighed.

So... I wanted to... apologize. For yelling at you last night.

Duncan turned his eyes away from the rising sun to look at her.

Whiski studied him. His eyes looked so different sometimes. It was like they belonged to someone much older (and she swore they kept changing between different shades of gold). Whiski waited for a response from the young tom for a couple seconds, but her impatience got the best of her.

Well! Aren't you going to say something?

Duncan turned back to face the sun. A tiny smile broke across his face.

You didn't apologize for trying to bite my tail off.

Whiski surprised herself by smiling back. *You are such a little kitten! I'm missing half my teeth!*

The ones you still have hurt!

Yeah, yeah... she coughed... *kitten.*

Am not!

Clearly, you are too. Whiski chuckled.

If I'm such a kitten, then... Duncan puffed up his chest. His ego was getting the better of him. *You won't mind if I challenge you to a race!*

A race? Whiski snorted. *That's kitten stuff.*

Duncan's brow furrowed.

Now, wrestling, boxing, stuff like that, that's what adult cats do. Whiski was trying hard not to burst out laughing. Boy cats, no matter their age, can never handle it when you challenge their physical prowess. She could tell that although Duncan was pleased she was talking to him, he was also clearly desperate to prove himself to her.

All right, all right, let's wrestle then, Duncan retorted in his best, whatever, no-big-deal voice.

Have you had any training? Whiski asked, a smirk on her face.

Duncan shrugged. *My mom taught me some stuff.*

Whiski smiled. *Well, we should probably start on the bed. You want padded surfaces when you're learning.*

I've wrestled tons of times, said Duncan nonchalantly.

Right... Whiski rolled her eyes. *Okay, so try not to wake the humans, they'll start throwing pillows. Consider their feet the edge of the ring. You take your stance. Legs crouched. No, not like that, like this. Good. Okay, now try to keep your balance with your tail, one paw up. Come on, claws out. You'll never be able to grab anything like that.*

Good. Now attack me.

Duncan was struck motionless by her words. They were the same ones his mother had used during his training.

Whiski studied his face and thought to herself, He must find me imposing, as well he should! *Don't have a hairball, Duncan, I won't hurt you... much.*

Duncan's attention snapped back to the present.

On three. One... two...

He gulped. A little flattery couldn't hurt.

You know, Whiski, you have very pretty white paws.

Pretty white paws? Whiski glared at him.

Yeah, you know, they're nice and uh... dainty? Duncan was running through adjectives in his head. Girls liked being called dainty, right?

A growl came from deep in Whiski's throat.

Oh dear...

Three!

"What the?" The human man muttered something about penguins in ice skates and the woman threw pillows in the direction of the dark ball of fur, claws, and fat bouncing at great speed across their bed.

~

Whiski yawned. *It's 8 a.m., and you've lost five rounds. You're done, kid.*

Duncan was breathing heavily. *I'm just wearing you down. Soon your age will kick in, and that's when I'll strike.* Whiski took her paw, wrapped it around Duncan's shoulder and flipped him hard through the air onto his back.

First, it's never wise to comment on a woman's age. And second, Whiski smirked; *It's not wise to tease someone who can take you down with one paw tied behind her back.*

Besides, she took her paw off his chest. *The humans will be up soon.* Whiski jumped down from the bed and headed toward the kitchen.

Duncan stayed on his back, exhausted. He groaned. He *was* a little kitten. Some Child of Sagira; he just got his tail handed to him by an 8-year-old girl cat! Then again, Whiski was clearly not what she appeared. They had that in common. Duncan exhaled gingerly. Even breathing was painful. Duncan pulled himself up and started to follow after her.

He spoke with a groan. *I thought for sure that they were going to get up when they started throwing pillows at us.*

Whiski shrugged. *Nah, not on the weekend. Besides, that's actually a normal human response to cat-wrestling.*

85

Duncan cocked his head. *Wait, a normal human response? How many humans have you known, anyway?*

Whiski stopped to fix her fur in the reflection of the oven door. She averted her eyes from his. *Come on, get up and clean your wounds. It takes practice, but you'll eventually learn how to defend yourself.*

Duncan rubbed his sore haunches. *Where did you learn this stuff anyway? I've never seen anyone fight like that.*

Whiski stifled a smile.

Duncan's stomach rumbled. He chose to let his previous questions go unanswered. The subject of her past was definitely still off limits. *I'm starving.*

Me too. Don't worry. If they don't get up in an hour or so we can start knocking things over in their bedroom.

Duncan froze, and his eyes widened. A gigantic orange cat was staring at them through the kitchen window. His muzzle was smashed so that his face was dominated by his two pale, watery yellow eyes.

Chapter 10

Whiski turned her head to look at Duncan. *What's your problem, kid?*

Duncan bolted past Whiski, and stood, growling defensively between her and the strange new cat.

Whiski turned, stunned by the little tom's actions. But life had taught her to react first and ask questions later, so she unleashed her claws and raised her hackles, ready to defend herself (and the little goober if necessary).

Whiski saw the orange cat and let her hackles drop and claws retract. She leapt up to the counter and flipped open the window lock. Whiski checked to make sure she could still hear the humans snoring softly, and she pushed the window open a crack.

The orange cat was laughing. *Looks like you've got a little bodyguard.*

Duncan's tail had plumed into a stick-straight, jet-black bottle brush.

Whiski turned to look back at her protector.

It's okay, Dunkelberry, Whiski stopped, immediately regretting the use of his nickname in front of the orange tomcat. *It's only Franklin.*

It's only Franklin? Whiski, I'm hurt.

Whiski ignored him. *What do you want, Franklin?*

Can't a neighbor say hello?

Duncan felt his hackles start to drop, but an entirely new sensation came over him. He intensely disliked Franklin.

And who is this little beast?

Whiski eyed Duncan, who was still glaring intensely at Franklin. *His name is Duncan, and he's generally quite friendly.* Whiski raised her eyebrow whiskers at Duncan and gestured with her head at Franklin.

Duncan grunted and nodded.

Whiski stepped in front of Duncan and spoke for the both of them. *So Franklin, did you have a reason for sneaking up on us, or were you just being your usual obnoxious self?*

Franklin smiled. *I meant no offense. I was just taking in the show through the screen here, but I'm afraid your little bodyguard... Dunkelberry, is it?... will require more training before he'll be useful to you.*

Duncan felt the heat rising into his ears, this time from embarrassment.

Whiski took a step toward Franklin.

He's actually not bad, Franklin. He could probably take you down. That is unless you crushed him under your purebred "stature." Whiski made a point to gesture at his ample fat as she emphasized the last word.

Fluffing his ruff defensively, Franklin set his eyes back on Duncan.

Well, you're clearly not from a decent breeding line. It looks like we have another little mixed-breed for the neighborhood. Interesting markings, Franklin frowned sarcastically, *but so terribly common. You do realize that every time another one of you moves in, the worse it looks for the rest of us? I swear, all these mixed-breeds...*

Duncan clenched his teeth. The heat across his face was spreading. If he only knew what breeding line Duncan came from.

I guess it's not your fault. You can't help how you came into this world.

The orange cat smiled satisfactorily at the reaction he was getting out of the young tom.

Whiski growled defensively. *Now wait just a minute! I told you I didn't want to hear any more of your purebred elitist crap in my house!*

Franklin nodded his head in mock deference. *Sorry, my dear, but the boy has to learn the truth sometime. Not all cats are created equal, and he might as well learn that sooner rather than later. I am a guardian of the pureblood line, and you two, well, you're an unintended byproduct of that line... tainted meat, if you will. Just be thankful that you have me to look out for the two of you.*

Get out! yelled Whiski.

Technically, I am out, replied Franklin smugly.

Whiski put her tiny black nose up against the window screen. Her white whiskers pressed through the small holes in the screen and brushed up against Franklin's face. *Frank, I swear if you don't walk away this instant, I'll tear right through this screen and turn you into my own personal pin cushion.*

Franklin turned his ample body around on the ledge, pushed forward, and landed with a satisfying thump on the grass

Such a temper. Not a surprise considering the alleys you were likely raised in, but, as a personal favor to you, I'll be on my way.

Turning, he continued across the open yard framed by a row of bushes. Rare form, Franklin, rare form, he thought to himself. That will teach them to mock me. He sighed. When will Whiski learn? He didn't say those things to be mean. It was simply the way of the world, and it was certainly that way for a reason. Cats like him were the guardians of their species. They didn't understand the enormous pressure he was under. He had a responsibility to take care of them. It was for their own good, and if they didn't understand that, well, then that was a sacrifice he must make. He looked up at the sun. He needed to move quickly. Brightly colored fall leaves rustled beneath him. The meeting would be starting soon. Franklin picked up his pace. The council was more important now than ever before. Quickly scanning the area around him, Franklin breathed a sigh of relief to see that no one was in sight. That was good. He didn't have time to waste this morning. He put his right paw underneath the fence and prepared for the pain and responsibility that came with his heritage. He felt a claw pierce lightly into the surface of his pad.

Do you bleed the blood of the pure?

Yes, whispered Franklin softly, *I bleed the blood that is pure.*

Then enter, brother.

As Franklin pulled his bleeding paw back from underneath the fence, a panel swung slightly to the side. He licked the blood from his paw. It would not do to waste pure blood. There was so little of it left anymore.

Chapter 11

Duncan's tail remained bristled long after Franklin had gone.

Whiski carefully closed the window before jumping back down to the kitchen floor. She let several minutes of silence pass between them, and then she surprised herself by briefly patting Duncan's shoulders.

You've got to let go of all that stuff Franklin said.

Duncan paced back and forth. *How do you ignore a cat like that? Who does he think he is? Calling us tainted!* Duncan felt his pulse throbbing behind his golden eyes which were slowly turning a dark bronze color.

Come here, gestured Whiski. She walked back into the kitchen to their food and water bowls. Duncan was still pacing as she dipped her paw deep into the cold water bowl and shook it sternly across Duncan's face.

Duncan inhaled sharply. *What? Why are you--?*

Whiski's whiskers curled into what Duncan was beginning to recognize as a smile. *You looked like you were about to combust.* She examined Duncan's dripping face. *Do you have some tabby in you?* She pretended to trace lines on his forehead. *I hear they have extraordinarily bad tempers, tabbies. Oh yes, I think that's a stripe. You're definitely part tabby with all that rage built up inside you.*

Duncan felt himself move from shock to anger back to shock, and finally to amusement. He narrowed his eyes, took a step forward, and dipped his paw in the bowl. Slicking his whiskers back, he purred, *How's this, my little mixed-breed beast?* Duncan struck his most arrogant pose, puffing out his still-inadequate teenage ruff. *Am I civilized yet?*

Whiski chuckled. *You do a pretty good Franklin, Dunkelberry.* She patted his paw with hers. *Try not to make it a habit. Now come on, the humans will be making breakfast soon, and I have much more to teach you.*

Teach me? Duncan was suddenly reminded of his sore muscles. *Will it be as painful as my first "lesson"?*

She rolled her eyes. *No, you big kitten, it won't all be painful, but you left your home at a young age, and there's a lot left for you to learn before you're fit to live with.*

Duncan's shoulders dropped. He was starting to wonder if her newfound interest in him was such a great thing after all.

Whiski snorted. *And you're not close to being done with wrestling lessons. You've got a long way to go, then there's boxing, stealth, etc...* her voice trailed off.

Duncan smiled thoughtfully. *Why are you doing all this for me?* Duncan placed a tentative paw on Whiski's shoulder but quickly pulled it back when he felt her stiffen.

Whiski paused outside the human bedroom door. That was a good question. Why was she doing this for him? Was it out of boredom? No, it was definitely more than that. She had planned on living out her years bathing in the sun and watching television. She studied his face out of the corner of her eye. This little boy cat had turned her quiet life with the married couple upside-down. And he was so like her brother, the same cocky walk, the same goofy smile, and the same stupid innocent and trusting nature... she'd hated him at first for that. Duncan had brought back memories she had thought were locked safely away with the rest of her heart. Now she had no idea why she was doing half the things she was doing. All she knew is that for the first time in a long time, it felt nice not to be alone.

Duncan cocked his head waiting for her answer, but he quickly realized she didn't have one for him, not yet.

Whiski indicated for Duncan to watch and learn. She stood outside of pillow range and uttered a guttural yowl in the direction of the queen bed. Within a couple yowls both cats recognized the familiar violent rustling of sheets in the human bed.

"Fine, fine, you win! We're up. We'll feed you. Just... shhh" grumbled the woman.

Duncan beamed proudly at Whiski. *You're good.*

~

Duncan spent the next six weeks having lessons with Whiski. When it seemed like they'd covered everything Duncan could have ever imagined a cat would need to know, Whiski would have a new lesson planned for him.

The first two weeks were focused on paw, tooth, and claw combat. Whiski showed him all kinds of things, like where to bite on the neck and torso to induce the most pain, how to gut an attacker with your back legs, how to throw a star-inducing stun-punch, and Duncan's favorite, how to throw your opponent. Duncan discovered quickly that Whiski's teaching style, while brutal, was straightforward and predictable. First, she would demonstrate the new move for Duncan. Then, they would alternate practicing the move on each another until he did it correctly. Once that happened, Whiski would make him repeat it until his technique became instinct. These sessions, though tedious, were incredibly effective. Duncan was finding himself growing stronger and more confident with each passing day.

As a change of pace, the third and fourth weeks were spent training Duncan in human manipulation. Whiski showed him how to get leftovers off the counter without getting caught. Unfortunately, the first time Duncan tried this, he left a grease trail of paw prints leading from the cast-iron skillet back to their window perch. Whiski made him lick up the paw prints while she ate the bacon scraps that he had retrieved. Duncan was bitter about this particular lesson, but there were definitely some upsides to her training. He could climb almost everywhere in the house now, he could secretly nab bits of deli turkey or slices of cheese from the human's plates, and he could make enough cute kitten faces and tortured cat yowls to make the human man and woman do practically anything he wanted. Duncan could tell Whiski was impressed by his overall progress (not that she'd ever tell him to his face). But he always knew she was pleased when she curled her white whiskers in satisfaction as he improved.

Whiski had also insisted that he learn much more than basic combat and survival techniques. Much to Duncan's dismay, week five was focused on teaching him cat etiquette.

This is stupid! Duncan growled. *No one needs to know this stuff!*

Whiski huffed. He could tell she was offended by his attitude. *You only got the basics from your mother! Sure, you know the rules for human interaction, but you eat like a truffle hound! Don't just stick your face in the bowl rooting around for anything to stuff in your kibble hole. Take small bites. Like this.* Whiski demonstrated on part of Duncan's breakfast.

I was going to eat that, you know. I'm a growing boy. Duncan grumbled defensively under his breath. *Besides, isn't it better for our cover for me to eat like an animal?*

Whiski rolled her eyes. *Yeah well, not any animal. You're not a dog.*

Duncan pretended to bark and let his tongue hang out. Whiski glared and pointed back to his bowl.

Duncan frowned. *Besides, you're not my mom, you're not supposed to teach me this kind of stuff.*

Whiski patted him on the head. *I'm old enough to be your mother, Dunkelberry.*

Duncan grinned. *Actually, you're much older than my mother. What does that make you? Like my grandmother?*

Whiski's eyes narrowed. *Fine, that's enough for now.* She twitched her short tail in annoyance. *You still need to learn stealth, though. You need to be able to hide at a moment's notice. Disappear into your surroundings. I saved that for last.*

Duncan shrugged. *I've got that covered.*

Whiski poked a claw at his belly fat. *Oh really? You know you're turning into quite the huge, and by huge, I mean fat, teenage tomcat. What are you according to the bathroom scale? Twelve pounds now? That's a lot of cat to hide...*

Duncan shifted his bulk. It was true that he had grown substantially over the past two months, but it was mostly muscle with just a touch of belly fat to make him look distinguished. He actually loved the fact that he was almost twice Whiski's weight. In another six months he'd be a grown tomcat that no one could boss around, not even bored middle-aged house cats.

Duncan waggled his butt in Whiski's face. *You know, I'm not exactly "Franklin-sized" yet.*

Whiski made a disgusted face while trying not to laugh. *Try to keep it that way, Dunkelberry.* She pulled herself up proudly. *You do know what weight I keep myself at...*

I know, I know, Duncan good-naturedly finished her sentence for her. *You keep yourself at a 7 lb fighting weight at all times.* He nudged Whiski playfully.

As they sat napping in the afternoon sun, Duncan couldn't believe how much things had changed between them.

After he'd left his mother and his siblings, he thought he'd never feel at home again. Whiski certainly hadn't welcomed him with open arms, but she'd definitely come around. He found her constant scowl endearing, and despite his whining, he enjoyed all their lessons together. She'd even decided to share her TV time with him as long as he promised to stay quiet during her soap operas (though she had no problem making fun of his shows). She still refused to talk about her past, but Duncan had stopped asking a long time ago. Whatever happened to her, she wasn't ready to share it with him. It was actually a relief. Whiski asked no questions of his past, and Duncan found that he could almost forget that he was a Son of Sagira. He still had frequent visions, but they were of boring, everyday things. No more flames. Duncan felt safe and normal.

Chapter 12

Duncan awoke with a start. It wasn't a vision. No, this was just a dream.

His mother had appeared to him. Duncan had run to her. As she held him tightly she whispered familiar words. *We cannot always control when the visions will come, and we cannot always control what the future will allow us to see. There are some things that we cannot see, no matter how hard we try. Be ready, Duncan, and be brave.* Duncan felt heat raging through every muscle, every fiber, and every pore of his body. Duncan cried out to Nellie in fear and in pain. She shook her head sadly. *I cannot help you now, my son. You are alone.* As she disappeared, Duncan burst into flames.

~

You okay, Dunkelberry? Whiski asked as they ate their breakfast the next morning.

Why? Duncan's heart began to race. What had he said? What had she heard?

No reason, you were just rolling around a lot in your dreams last night.

Duncan let a grim smile frame his tired face.

Everyone dreams.

Whiski frowned at the use of her own words against her.

She watched the young tom eating his breakfast. Something was clearly bothering him. His eyes were a dull dark gold, and his fur was a mess. He was shedding like crazy. That was certainly not normal cat behavior going into winter months.

I hope he's okay, thought Whiski to herself as she carefully chewed her meaty mush. She couldn't help it. She liked the kid, not that she'd ever tell him that. But his eyes looked, well, haunted. She knew what it was like to be haunted by dreams. Whiski felt a small shudder run down her spine as the two of them continued to eat alongside each another in silence. She turned her gaze back to her bowl to avoid making him more uncomfortable than he already was. But she couldn't help but wonder. What does he have to be haunted about?

~

Duncan's mouth dropped open, and several pieces of half-chewed kibble fell to the floor.

Whiski scowled. *Seriously, that's just a waste of good food.*

Duncan ignored her and whispered out of the corner of his mouth. *What... is... that?* He gestured with his tail at the falling white powder slowly collecting outside the window.

Whiski turned, her eyes got large, and her tail began to rotate excitedly.

It's snow! I hadn't even noticed. It's early this year! She looked back at Duncan to see his mouth still hanging open.

You've never seen snow, have you? Whiski chuckled. *That's what you get for only watching all those spaceship sci-fi shows; you'll never learn anything about the real world. No snow in space, Dunkelberry.*

Duncan raised his eyebrow whiskers, grinned, and trotted quickly over to the window and stood up on his hind legs. He pressed his paws to the glass.

Whoa! It's cold! The window is freezing! Whiski, come feel!

Whiski chuckled and rolled her eyes. *That's the idea.* She joined him next to the window. *Check this out.* She breathed warm air onto the window and put her white-socked paw to the glass. Whiski slowly spread her claws and lightly outlined her paw. She smiled thoughtfully. *My mom used to call these snow tigers.*

Duncan listened quietly. Whiski continued. *I was born in the winter, right before Christmas actually. So when I was young, my brother...* she stopped for a second, weighing whether she wanted to continue. She did. *My brother used to tease me that I had such tiny paws that I was making snow bunnies, not tigers.*

Duncan watched as Whiski stared out the window. She looked younger and happier than he'd ever seen her. She had a distant smile on her face, and her big green eyes were soft and absent of the piercing sharpness that her gaze so often carried.

He breathed heavily against the glass, letting the moisture stick. Duncan placed his paw on the glass. It was already much bigger than Whiski's. *Like this?* Duncan asked as he extended his paw to draw on his claws.

Yes, not too much claw, lightly at the end, Whiski laughed. *Dunkelberry, you do have huge paws.*

Duncan smiled, *That's why I make a good tiger.* He reared his head back and did a tiger roar.

Whiski laughed. *I don't know. I'm not sure it looks like a snow tiger. It's too big,* she teased, pretending to seriously evaluate the paw print. *Hmm, maybe more like a bear... a really fat bear.*

Duncan poked Whiski with his tail. *You're just jealous, snow bunny.*

Whiski snorted and let her breath fog the glass to reveal their two prints.

You're a lot like my brother, Duncan.

Duncan stared at their prints and back at Whiski. Then it hit him. She trusted him. He looked at their foggy reflection and smiled. He wanted to tell his mother that she'd been wrong. He would always be different, but that didn't mean he would have to spend the rest of his life alone. Duncan took a deep breath and tried to fully absorb the feel and the smell of the world around him. He refused to be haunted by visions and dreams. Whiski's voice pulled at him.

You know what my favorite thing is about winter?

Duncan shook his head. *Not snow?* He asked.

Heaters.

Heaters?

Yeah, the man and the woman start turning on those big vents all around the house. Whiski paused. *Ooh, I bet they've got the office one on low already! That room is always the coldest. If you lean off the desk you can actually turn it up with your paws!* She moved quickly down the hallway, talking over her shoulder and expecting Duncan to follow.

He dutifully did.

Whiski stopped in front of a large, blowing vent. *Oh yeah, it's on. Feel this.* Whiski stuck her nose within several inches of the grate and let the heat blow softly against her fur. She jumped up to the desk and turned up the heater. She whispered out of the corner of her mouth. *The man always thinks it's the woman who turns it up.* She grinned and jumped down to sit back in front of the heater.

You try, she gestured with her eyes closed in Duncan's direction.

Duncan stuck his face forward. The heat felt wonderful.

Don't lean too far forward. This thing will burn your nose.

Duncan felt himself drifting forward. It was like he was experiencing the heat from the inside as well as from the outside. Like two halves meeting, Duncan leaned further forward. He could feel his whiskers begin to singe, but he was far from caring.

Whiski's nose was the first of her senses to alert her to the fact that something was terribly wrong. It smelled like burning fur.

Duncan, back up! Whiski yowled.

Duncan's eyes were a deep copper, and they glowed like metal changing colors in a forge.

Duncan! Whiski reached out to push him away from the heater, but his fur burned her paws to the touch.

She wrenched her body back at the sight of him. He was covered in glowing white-hot flames. They licked across his body everywhere but his feet and on the small white diamond on his chest.

DUNCAN!

It was like he was in a trance. He must be in shock, Whiski thought to herself. What do I do? Think, Whiski, think! If he moves, he could set the whole house on fire! Her eyes rapidly scanned the office for anything she could use to stop the flames from consuming him.

The man! He'd left his fast-food drink on his desk! Whiski leapt up to the desk and spun to kick the sweating soft drink cup with her back paws. A wave of soda and melted ice crashed down in Duncan's direction.

As soon as the liquid hit Duncan, he began to change colors until his black fur was left with only a tinge of red. It was a mark that he would carry for the rest of his life.

Whiski raced down from the desk. He'd be burned badly. She needed to get him help, she...

DUNCAN! Whiski yelled.

He'd collapsed on the floor, and his fur... wait, his fur... he had... fur.

Whiski's voice began to shake. *Duncan?*

Chapter 13

Duncan regained his feeling before he regained his sight. He was lying muzzle down in a brown, sticky pool of liquid. What had happened?

The last thing he remembered was slipping into the deep darkness of the heat. He tried to move his limbs. They were tingling. He pushed up and fell back down.

His stomach lurched and he vomited hot blood and kibble onto the carpet.

Whiski? He croaked.

Nothing. No answer, just the steady whir of the heater.

Duncan tried to push himself up again, this time more slowly. The room spun less violently and then he saw her. She was crouched on the top of the desk with her back against the wall. Her hackles were up.

Duncan couldn't hide the fear in his voice. Something was very wrong. *Whiski? What happened?*

He moved a step toward her. She took a small step back and hissed.

Stay back! She growled.

Duncan's eyes widened and then narrowed.

Whiski, calm down and tell me exactly what happened.

You're one of them, aren't you? She shook her head, but she kept her eyes fixed on him.

Duncan felt his heart catch in his throat.

What are you talking about?

You burst into flames, Duncan! You should be dead!

You must have... Duncan's mind was reeling along with his stomach. He was only supposed to have one power. That's what his mother had told him. None since Sagira herself had ever possessed more than one of her powers. The fear in Whiski's eyes pierced through him and brought him back to the present. *You must have seen something wrong.* Duncan searched his mind for an explanation that would make sense, but there wasn't one.

You're one of the cursed! You're a Son of Sagira! Whiski's voice was picking up volume. *Don't lie!*

It was in this moment that Duncan made a decision that would alter the entire course of his life. He should blind her. He knew that. His mother had warned him that this day would come. But as he looked at Whiski and the fear and anger that dominated her eyes, he couldn't. She was his friend and the only family he had now. It wasn't that he didn't want to erase all the hatred and disgust that she was directing toward him, but he couldn't do it to her. He wouldn't do it to her. So there he was, left standing in a pool of soda and vomit with nothing but the truth to offer her.

But the truth was that he had no idea what was happening to him.

~

Duncan could hear the sound of the man and woman fidgeting with their keys outside the front door.

He didn't have much time left.

Whiski, we need to talk. I have something to tell you.

Whiski's eyes narrowed. *There's nothing to talk about. You're a freak, and you're a liar. My first reaction to you was the right one. You're nothing but trouble!*

Duncan's ears fell back. *I know you're angry, but please give me a chance to explain. I'm still me. I'm still Duncan!*

Both cats' ears flicked toward the sound of the front door opening.

Quiet, Whiski hissed. *The humans are coming.*

The man pushed open the office door and immediately dropped his jacket and keys at the scene that lay before him.

"Honey!" The man bellowed. "I need your help in here!"

Duncan could hear the woman kicking the front door shut and the sound of crinkly plastic grocery bags being set down.

"Okay!" She yelled back. "Just a second!"

"No! Now!" The man replied urgently. "It's the cats. Something's happened!"

Duncan could hear the sound of the woman's feet slapping against the floor as she ran to join her husband in the office doorway.

"Quick! Get him in a towel, call the vet! We'll get the carpet later!"

Within seconds, Duncan felt himself being scooped up and wrapped tightly in a bath towel and carried off to the bathroom by the man. He hadn't realized that he was trembling.

Duncan could hear the woman describing the contents of his vomit into her cell phone. She sounded panicked. Duncan felt a twinge of guilt as well as anger. What was happening to him? He'd blown everything. Whiski knew who he was--even if she knew nothing about his power of sight, she'd certainly witnessed him explode into a ball of flames. And the humans, they had definitely noticed that something was wrong. But the worst part was that he didn't have the foggiest idea of how to make any of it right again.

Duncan let himself go limp in the man's arms. After a few minutes the woman reappeared. "The vet said we should bathe him and monitor him over the next 24 hours for changes in behavior. He said it could have been another seizure." She wiped her forehead with the back of her hand. "He also said that the blood in the vomit could have just been a broken blood vessel, but that it was important to keep an eye on him." The woman stroked Duncan's head tenderly. "My poor baby, we'll get you cleaned up, and you'll feel much better." The man adjusted his hold to curl Duncan more tightly into his chest. Duncan mewed softly as the woman began to draw a bath. Whiski was nowhere to be found.

Duncan allowed himself to be washed. There was no point in struggling. He was a mess, and he could only imagine how pitiful he looked. He watched as the water turned a murky color from the soda in his fur.

He needed time to think. How would he ever begin to explain what was happening to Whiski, when he didn't fully understand it himself? Besides, even if he could explain it, there was no way of knowing if she would hear him out. It had taken her days to even speak to him, and that was before he'd burst into flames.

Duncan hung his head. The humans were towel-patting him dry now. The woman had tried to use a hairdryer on a low setting, but Duncan thought it was way too close to the sensation of the floor heater. After several warning scratches, the humans had decided to proceed with towels only. They wrapped him in a new towel every 10 minutes as they waited for his coat to return to normal.

"Does his coat look different to you?" The woman asked her husband as she stared quizzically at Duncan's fur.

"No. Why? Did we not get all the soda out?"

The woman stroked Duncan's ears. "No, it just looks a little more reddish now. I guess it must be the lighting in here."

Her husband chuckled. "He looks like an ordinary black cat to me, Honey."

Duncan rolled his eyes. Well, at least the man wasn't suspicious.

The woman smiled at her husband. "How's the rest of him doing?"

The man felt Duncan's coat under the towel. "I think he's dry enough now." He set Duncan down and patted his head. "Now, go see Whiski. You gave her quite a scare."

Duncan grimaced. He had no idea.

Chapter 14

Duncan spent the rest of the day trying to get Whiski alone to talk to her, but not only was Whiski keeping to herself, Duncan was being constantly followed by his two highly neurotic human caretakers. He couldn't even go to the bathroom without the woman immediately examining his poo for signs of distress.

Frustrated, Duncan pulled himself onto their queen bed. He licked his paw and rubbed it across his temple. He was exhausted and his body ached intensely. He would have to wait until night-time. The humans would be asleep, and he could safely approach Whiski without causing a scene.

Duncan felt his golden eyes growing heavy as he placed a paw over them. Yes, tonight he would talk to Whiski. He had to find a way to make her understand that he wasn't something to be afraid of. At least he didn't think he was something to be afraid of...

~

Duncan's eyes snapped open. It was late. He looked at the clock. Well after midnight. The humans had moved him to the foot of the bed. He rose stiffly and scanned the room for Whiski. She wasn't in her usual place. He hopped down to the floor. *I bet she's afraid I'll set the bed on fire*, he muttered to himself. He shook his head. He shouldn't joke. Whiski had witnessed something terrifying, and he, sadly enough, was that something. Duncan checked the office. Nothing. He checked the bathroom. Nothing. He could feel his anxiety building. What could he possibly say to make things right?

Duncan walked quietly into the living room. Everything about the way the moonlight filtered through the air reminded him of the night his mother had told him the truth about who he was. He was just as nervous tonight as he had been then, perhaps even more so. At least at his old house he had his mother to guide him. This time he was alone.

He could see Whiski was staring out the window. Her eyes were only half open.

Duncan cleared his throat with a small rumble. *Couldn't sleep?*

Whiski stiffened and hissed in surprise. *What are you doing sneaking up on me like that?*

Duncan raised his paw in an attempt to show he was sorry. *I wasn't sneaking up on you. I just wanted to talk.*

Whiski glared down at him and said nothing.

Duncan twitched his tail uncomfortably. He wasn't sure how to begin. *I'm sorry about today. I didn't know that was going to happen, and I didn't mean to scare you.*

Whiski let a skeptical huff escape her nose.

Duncan continued and tried to strengthen his shaky voice. *Look. I know you don't trust me, but I'm going to tell you everything... the truth about me, because you're my family, and even if you hate my guts, you need to hear what I have to say.*

Whiski turned her head to stare back into the night, but Duncan could tell she was still watching him out of the corner of her eye.

Fine, you don't have to look at me, Duncan said in a tired voice. *I know you can hear me.*

He kept his eyes fixed on Whiski. *I am one of the Children of Sagira. I was born with the power of sight.* Duncan could see one of her tiny black ears cock back in surprise. He wondered what she already knew about the Children of Sagira. What stories had she been told, if any? *It started when I was very young. I could see things before they happened. I had visions, dreams, of the future. They were powerful at first. I passed out the first time it happened.* Whiski's eyes were hard and fiercely bright in the moonlight. Duncan paused, hoping that Whiski would say something. She didn't. *What I'm trying to tell you is that I didn't know today would happen. My mother has the power of sight, and I have the power of sight. I would never in a million years have guessed that this could happen... the fire... it shouldn't have happened.* Duncan shook his head. *I know it's crazy, and I don't know how else to explain this to you, but I swear that I'm still the same cat I was when you met me.*

Whiski whispered, *I didn't like you then.*

Duncan's ears fell back. There was so much hate in her voice.

Whiski continued looking out the window. She spoke quietly, *I didn't* think your kind still existed. *I thought you had been hunted to extinction during the Dark Times.* Her voice was cold. *I thought that you were just stories told at night to scare kittens.*

Duncan's voice was defensive. *Well, I am real, all right! I didn't ask for this!*

Whiski was quiet.

His hurt turned quickly to anger. *You know, I thought you'd understand! I thought the fact that I told you the truth would mean something. My siblings never even knew what I was! I broke an oath to my mother that I would never tell another soul about me, but I'm telling you everything because I trust you and I care about you. We're family.* Duncan's voice was shaking. *I thought you were my friend, Whiski, and that you'd always be my friend. What are you so afraid of?* Duncan took a step forward and spoke up at her, *I would never hurt you.*

Whiski whirled around to face Duncan. She couldn't it take anymore. Fear and anger poured out of her. *Never hurt me? How can someone like you even say something like that? Cats like you are responsible for centuries of fear and hate directed toward all of us.* Whiski leapt down from the window and let her furious green eyes meet with Duncan's. *You lied to me about what you are, and you know what, I can understand that. But Duncan, what I can't understand is how you are trying to sit here in front of me and tell me you would never hurt me! The Children of Sagira are liars and traitors and nothing, nothing, good has ever come of them. You are a danger to everyone in this house, and I will not let you destroy my life or my humans' lives! You asked me what I am afraid of. I'm afraid of you!*

Duncan felt like she'd raked him in the face with her claws. He could feel the anger building inside him. He jumped up to the windowsill. *My mother and I, we'd never hurt anyone! It's not like that! I'm not a traitor, and I would never hurt you or our humans!*

Whiski hissed. Her eyes were only a few inches from his. *Fine! Say I believed you! What about the fire? I've never heard of any cat since Sagira to hold more than one of her powers. What are you?*

Duncan growled in frustration. His eyes were growing darker. *I DON'T KNOW! I DON'T KNOW WHO, OR WHAT, I AM, ALL RIGHT? DOES THAT MAKE YOU HAPPY?*

Whiski took a step back. *No, that doesn't make me happy. What would make me happy is if you had never come here.*

Duncan was breathing heavily. *I didn't ask to come here either, but I did.*

Whiski jumped down and Duncan followed. She dipped her paw in their water bowel and splashed him. Duncan stumbled backward, rubbing his wet face. His eyes returned to their normal bright gold.

How do you plan on controlling yourself? She hissed.

Duncan didn't reply.

I said, how do you plan on controlling yourself in front of the humans?

Duncan flicked his tail in frustration. *I don't know. That was the first time it ever happened. My mother is the one who taught me how to control my visions. I don't know how to control the fire!*

Whiski's face remained emotionless. *You have two powers. How do we know it will stop there?*

Duncan was struck silent by the thought. *I guess... I guess I hadn't thought about that yet.*

Whiski growled. *Well, start thinking. You need to be able to control yourself. You're a danger to all of us the way you are right now. You've heard Franklin talk about his purebred guard. If Franklin, or any cat who thinks like Franklin, ever saw you, they'd report you in the twitch of a whisker!* Whiski's tail was snapping angrily back and forth. *What you don't seem to understand is that if we don't keep you hidden from the humans and from other cats, we'll all pay the price.*

Duncan had not prepared himself for the turn their conversation had taken. *What do you mean, turn me in?*

Whiski didn't answer, and instead jumped back to her window. *And if you put even one paw out of line, so help me, I will make you sorry. I don't care who you are, or how powerful you are. I won't let you hurt this family.*

"This family" she had said. *Whiski,* Duncan paused for a long time, *Are we still family?* His voice broke as he spoke.

Whiski sighed and turned her face to look out the window.

No, Duncan. We're not.

Chapter 15

The corner of Franklin's mouth curled up in a sneer. The two mixed-breeds had no idea they were being watched. It was a shame that he couldn't hear what they were talking about. They were clearly having a heated argument. So emotional. Franklin laughed to himself. And to think, just yesterday they were the best of friends. Mixed-breeds didn't have the first idea of what it meant to be loyal.

Franklin had an excellent view into the windows of the houses around him. The girl cat and the young tom couldn't see into his home, but he could easily see into theirs. It was perfect. He curled his ginger body up so that the warm air of the vent kept him from catching cold. There was still snow outside. That would make their meeting decidedly more difficult. No matter, it was the third Sunday of the month, and that meant that the council would be meeting today before dawn.

Franklin cleaned his claws in disgust. He would have to report on activities of interest within his territory. There was nothing much to tell.

The young mixed-breed tom and the middle-aged girl cat were exceedingly boring to watch. Clearly he had missed some falling out between the two cats. No matter, he was sure it was over something mundane. Franklin turned to check the time on the grandfather clock ticking in the hallway. It was still several hours before it would be time to leave. There was time yet for a nap.

~

Five strokes of the clock. Franklin straightened his fur and pushed his way out of his cat door. My word, it was cold!

Franklin moved quickly through the snow, carefully covering his tracks with his large plush tail. It would not do to be late, but Franklin also knew the council would not approve of his leaving a marked trail that could be followed.

He approached the fence and placed his paw underneath the panel.

Do you bleed the blood of the pure?

Yes, I bleed the blood that is pure.

Then enter, brother.

Franklin licked his bleeding paw and placed it back in the snow. The cold provided instant relief.

A small Persian held the panel for him. She had a dark, smoky-chocolate coat and the same pale, watery yellow eyes as Franklin.

You're late, Franklin.

Franklin glared. *Vera, you know I must travel farther than the others.*

Vera swung the panel back quickly. *Then you should leave earlier, brother.*

Franklin grunted. *Has the meeting begun?*

Not yet, but we must hurry. You are the last one to come.

The two cats walked skillfully, though Franklin less so, through a row of holly bushes. Vera pushed open the tiny basement window and slid through easily. Franklin followed but had to struggle to pull his haunches through the small frame.

A circle of cats had formed in the room below them. It was a large, dark room with ornate leather furniture and richly colored patterned rugs. A small wet bar marked one corner, a pool table the other. The air was scented with the heavy smell of potpourri and cigars.

A long, lean Siamese cat pointed with her tail in Franklin's direction and whispered something to the Cornish Rex next to her. They giggled, none too discretely.

Franklin gathered his bulk and walked quickly alongside Vera.

We've been waiting, Franklin, said a low voice from the head of the circle.

Franklin bowed. *I apologize, Varik. I meant no offense. I simply wished to ensure that my tracks were covered so that none could follow.* A tall, muscular Abyssinian stepped forward. His fur was coarse and ruddy, a deep golden color, ticked with red.

Varik studied the Persian carefully for what felt like a very long time to Franklin.

You are forgiven, Franklin. Let us begin. Vera, we shall start with you. The chocolate Persian bowed and moved to the center of the circle.

118

Varik nodded at her. *Tell us what you know.*

And so for the next hour, each cat reported on his or her territory, all speaking with disdain about the activities of the mixed-breeds that they watched so diligently.

Soon it was Franklin's turn, and he shared with the council what he knew of his mixed-breeds. He spoke of Whiski's training of Duncan, their growing friendship, and their apparent fight that evening. The other cats snickered as they listened

With one look from his powerful green eyes, Varik silenced them. *We do not laugh at those less fortunate than us.*

The other cats hung their heads. Varik let them sit in uncomfortable silence before he continued. *I am a descendent of the Abyssinian line, the Abyssinians who first began life with the humans in ancient Egypt, the Abyssinians who rose up against the Children of Sagira when they grew selfish and corrupt, the Abyssinians who helped to cleanse the world of those who brought such destruction and hatred toward our kind.* He paused for effect. *I come from the line of Abyssinians who, along with your ancestors, began this council and set down the laws for life with humans so that we may never see such fear and death again. I do not say these things to boast. I say these things because our ancestors did not do this without sacrifice. We must be diligent. Our blood is pure, and so must be our purpose. We must keep the balance.* Varik paused again, letting the weight of his words sink in. *We are here to protect the mixed-breeds from themselves. They do not know any better. We do. This is the sacred duty passed down to us. We are to watch over them. We are to make sure the Children of Sagira never rise again. We are the guardians of all felines.*

Varik turned his majestic ruddy body and bowed at each of the purebred cats to signal the end of the meeting. As each cat left, one at a time, Varik gestured for Franklin to stay back. Once they had all left, Varik spoke. *Franklin, I wish to speak with you in private.*

Franklin lowered his head nervously. *Yes, Varik.*

I want you to follow these two mixed-breeds more closely. Shadow them. You will report back to the council in one month. I want more information on this young tomcat. There is something peculiar about him.

Franklin had no idea what Varik was talking about, but it was not his place to ask questions. He whispered. *Yes, Varik. As you wish.*

Franklin.

Yes, Varik?

Don't disappoint me.

Chapter 16

Whiski continued to stare out the window long after Duncan had left.

Her heart was beating rapidly from all the emotions still drumming around in her chest. She could feel her claws digging into the soft painted wood of the window frame.

Whiski exhaled. She was exhausted. So much had changed during the course of a day.

She was sharing her home with a very dangerous cat, and from what she knew of the Children of Sagira, and that was very little, if she made him angry enough, he could easily kill her before she could raise a paw to defend herself. His kind was to be feared. No matter his intentions, it was what he was, a curse on whoever's life he touched.

Whiski let out a dry laugh. When she was a kitten, she'd heard bedtime stories about the Children of Sagira. She'd thought her mother had made them up as a way to keep her and her siblings out of trouble. "Be good, or the Children of Sagira will find you," her mother used to say. Whiski smiled grimly. Apparently she had not been good.

Whiski turned to make sure that Duncan had left the room. It had taken her most of the day to come to grips with what she'd seen in the office. At first she'd try to make herself believe she hadn't seen it, not really. Duncan hadn't burst into flames and miraculously recovered. Whiski's paws trembled at the memory. Duncan lying in the pool of soda, writhing in his unconsciousness. Today she'd realized that everything she'd ever been told about the Children of Sagira was true. Whiski muttered to herself, *That kind of knowledge is enough to knock you flat on your back.* She shut her eyes. Duncan had been lying to her since the day he first entered their, no, since he entered *her* home. Whiski angrily kicked over a bucket of cat toys and began to pick apart a stuffed mouse. She'd been such a fool to trust him!

Duncan watched silently as Whiski ripped apart the first mouse and then selected a second. He had hidden himself in the shadows of the living room. He had been there for hours, motionless. He had a new and deeper understanding of panic and loneliness than he'd ever thought possible, and it had paralyzed him. Duncan decided that Whiski must not realize that he was watching her. He was sure that there was no way she would ever have let him witness the frustration and emotion that was spilling out of her right now. She was far too proud to have done this in front of him, even before she'd found out what he was. Duncan laid his head down in despair. Whiski would only hate him more if he revealed himself now, a witness to her feelings. Feelings that couldn't be bottled up or controlled any longer. Duncan's eyes began to close. The last thing he saw was Whiski tearing what was left of a plush mouse into tiny pieces.

~

Duncan found himself slipping into the blackness of sleep and then into the familiar blackness of the fur that surrounded his mother's deep golden eyes. She was afraid.

Duncan stretched out his paw to touch his mother's. They were almost the same size now, only her paw was trembling.

Mom, it'll be okay, reassured Duncan, but he couldn't shake the fear in her eyes when she looked at him. *We'll figure it out. But please, you have to tell me where to go.*

Duncan watched as Nellie let go of his paw.

Not with her here, she pointed in disgust with her tail at Whiski. Wait, Duncan couldn't believe it! Whiski was with them? What was she doing here?

Nellie stared off into the night. Duncan let the silence hang between them. He looked pleadingly at Whiski, who then rolled her eyes, hissed a few curse words in Nellie's direction and stomped off to wait outside.

And then, as if she were steering a great ship out to sea, Nellie changed course and took a step toward Duncan.

Duncan.

Yes, Mom?

I need you to look at me, just like when you were little. I need you to bring your eyes level with mine. Look at me.

Duncan hesitated.

Nellie gave her son a tight smile. *Trust me.*

Duncan let his golden eyes lock with hers.

What do you see?

~

Duncan felt an object hit him squarely between the eyes.

What the--?

A small plush mouse lay on the floor beside him. The sun had overtaken his corner, and it was now mid-morning.

You were talking in your sleep, Whiski scowled. The humans are awake. *I had to shut you up before you called too much attention to yourself.*

Duncan rubbed the sore spot on the bridge of his nose where the mouse had made contact.

You could have tapped me on the shoulder, he muttered, *I won't bite.*

Whiski's eyes narrowed. *I didn't want to risk burning my paws again.*

Duncan met her glare. *Very funny.*

I wasn't trying to be funny...

Duncan huffed. *Have the humans put out our breakfast?*

Whiski shrugged.

Duncan could barely contain his frustration. *So first you pelt me in the face with a mouse to wake me up, and now you refuse to speak to me?*

Whiski leapt up to perch on top of the couch.

Duncan grumbled some choice words he'd heard on television.

He inhaled deeply. The humans must be cooking. It smelled like meat and fat sizzling in a pan.

Duncan moved faster. Yes, the human woman was indeed making bacon!

"Well, hi there, Dunkelberry! How are you feeling today? Better?" The woman bent down to scratch his head.

Duncan's nostrils flared as he took in the scent. If only their kibble and mush smelled like that.

"Sorry, Duncan. No bacon for kitties. Would you like some wet food?"

Duncan looked at the woman longingly as she opened the fridge.

No, he thought seriously at the woman, *I'd like your food. Two slices of bacon to go, please.*

The woman blinked several times and put the can of meaty mush back in the fridge.

Duncan's mouth hung open as he watched her place two pieces of bacon on the floor.

No way!

She turned back to the pan and resumed cooking the remaining bacon.

Duncan looked questioningly over his shoulder. He could hardly believe what had just happened. He looked warily from side to side, picked up the bacon between his teeth, and dashed back to the living room before the woman could change her mind.

Whiski's eyes widened when she saw Duncan dragging the strips of bacon into the room. She dove down from the couch and grabbed Duncan by the scruff and held on tightly.

What did you do? Did you hurt her? She growled, her mouth full of his fur and skin.

Duncan wrenched himself free.

No! She just gave them to me!

You're lying! Humans don't just hand out bacon! What did you do?

Duncan lowered his voice. *I just...* and then it hit him. *I asked for two pieces, and she gave them to me.*

Whiski took a step back.

Just like that?

Just like that.

Whiski whispered almost inaudibly, *You have the power of persuasion...*

I... Duncan struggled to speak, *I didn't mean to! It was an accident. I didn't know!*

Both cats sat frozen in shock when the woman entered the room.

"Duncan! Whiski! How'd you get that bacon?"

Both cats stared blankly up at the woman.

"Naughty kitties!" scolded the woman as she lifted the bacon strips up off the carpet.

Duncan waited for the woman to turn the corner.

Wow...

Whiski growled. *Don't you get any ideas!* Duncan noticed she had backed up a few more steps.

Duncan stared in confusion until he realized the source of her fear.

I wouldn't do that to you! And I only accidentally did it to our human!

Whiski's right ear twitched back skeptically.

Duncan's tail dropped. *I'm not a monster. I'm just...* Duncan couldn't finish the sentence. The truth was that he didn't know anymore.

The rest of the weekend passed uneventfully. Whenever Duncan began to feel himself heating up, he'd dip his tail into their water bowl or sit in the human bathroom sink and turn the water on. He kept to himself, and Whiski kept both her eyes on Duncan.

But Duncan was restless. He needed answers. What was happening to him? And that vision. How could he forget the vision of his mother and the fear in her eyes? What was she trying to show him? And besides, how could the vision be real, their paths had changed, hadn't they? His old home felt so far away, yet he wanted nothing more than to speak to his mother again. But he had no idea where his mother was, and he had no idea where to start looking.

~

As soon as the humans had shut the door on Monday morning, Whiski had grabbed Duncan by the scruff again. She let go hastily.

I'm very concerned.

That's sweet of you.

Whiski hissed. *This is serious, Duncan! You're unstable! Why,* Whiski stammered, she was hyperventilating, *Why, you could force the humans to eat bacon for every meal, and before you know it., they'd have heart attacks... And we'd have to move... And the house would burn down!*

Duncan raised his eyebrow whiskers. *You've been thinking about this a lot, haven't you?*

Duncan's response was enough to force Whiski to gain control of herself.

All right, she muttered, *So maybe that wasn't the best example.*

Duncan forced himself not to smile.

But you're still dangerous. You need help, Duncan. You can't stay here, not like this.

Duncan's jaw clenched. As much as he wanted to, he couldn't deny it.

I think, Duncan paused to gather his thoughts, *I think I know what I'm supposed to do.*

Whiski's eyebrows furrowed. *What do you mean?*

I had a vision. I was talking to my mother. She... well, she showed me something, something important about who I am.

What'd she show you?

I don't know.

What do you mean you don't know?

You hit me in the face with a mouse before I could find out!

Whiski smirked and then shrugged. *Fair enough. So now what do you do? How are you supposed to find your mother?*

Duncan paused and then looked into Whiski's fierce green eyes.

I think you're supposed to help me.

Chapter 17

Duncan waited for Whiski to stop laughing.

No, really? Whiski held her paw over her stomach while she tried to catch her breath. *What's your plan?*

Duncan frowned and directed what he hoped was a disapproving look at Whiski. *I saw you in my vision. We're supposed to visit my mother together. She must know something that can help us.*

Whiski's whiskers dropped, and the laughter drained from her face.

You are *serious. Wow...* Whiski stared at the carpet as she tried to make sense of what she was hearing. *No.*

What do you mean, no? protested Duncan.

I know what's out there, and it's too dangerous. I won't go through it again.

Duncan's voice lost its edge. *Did you live outside on your own before*

129

our humans?

Whiski's eyes hardened. *Forget it, Duncan. You're on your own.* She turned and started walking toward the kitchen.

Whiski, wait, hold on. Duncan quickly followed after her.

Whiski continued.

Just help me get out. Help me find a way to my mother's. I won't ask you to come with me.

Whiski paused. *What about your vision?*

My visions, well, they can be changed. Duncan shuddered at the memory of Anna and the foosball table. His voice faltered. *It's just that I have no idea where to look. I can feel it, the changes, the energy inside of me. It's building, and I need to figure out what's happening to me.* Duncan's golden eyes darkened. *You were right. I can't stay here.*

Whiski's shoulders sank.

Besides, you're the only... Duncan exhaled sadly. Whiski had made it clear that they weren't family anymore... and maybe they never had been. Duncan started again. *You're the only one who can help me.*

Whiski looked down at her paws. She couldn't believe what she was about to do.

What was their last name?

Who?

The human family who helped raise you. Do you know their last name?

So you'll help me? Duncan thought he could cry with relief.

130

Well, not if you don't tell me their name.

Duncan smiled gratefully. *Luther. They were the Luther family.*

Whiski turned her head so that Duncan could see her profile. Her white whiskers framed her petite black face. She signaled with a nod of her head for Duncan to follow.

Have you ever used a computer, Duncan?

Duncan shook his head. *No, my mother said that they were too risky to use. She said the humans might catch us.*

Whiski snorted. *Well, she was right about that, but they have their uses.*

~

Franklin watched with curious eyes from his perch in his family's tree. *Blasted, Varik!* It was freezing outside. He tried to suppress a surge of guilt. He shouldn't complain. It was his job to follow orders and be as vigilant as Varik thought necessary. But for the life of him, he couldn't figure out what was so interesting about these two mixed-breeds. Franklin rubbed his watery eyes with his paw and frowned at the state of his claws. Everything had taken a backseat to this tedious assignment. Varik had threatened... no, Varik had honored him with this task. Varik, who was both wise and brave. Franklin, had no right to question his authority. It was Varik who had given his life meaning again.

He let a bitter rumble escape from his chest. It was true that he had once dreamt of having a family. As a purebred, one's sole purpose is to breed, to raise a family, to continue one's bloodline. But no, Franklin had been found to be "less than acceptable" for breeding, something about his eyes. He glared down at the two mixed-breeds who were once

131

again having another heated discussion.

Franklin shook his head. He must stay focused. He had wasted years of his life in bitter regret before Varik had come. Franklin let a thin smile frame his smashed face. He remembered when he'd first heard of the guard. His sister, Vera, had approached him on Varik's behalf. A new guard had been formed in their territory where purebreds watched over the mixed-breeds and ferals in their area. Each member had sworn a blood oath to Varik to watch over those beneath them and to ensure that the rules for cat-human interaction were enforced. The job required a great deal of stealth and secrecy. Franklin puffed up his chest proudly. It was not always easy to be stealthy as a 20-pound orange Persian, but he had done so.

As Varik always said, *Order is best maintained when those beneath you don't know who is watching them, only that they are being watched.*

~

Whiski stopped Duncan. *Grab the curtains.*

What, why? asked Duncan.

Whiski grabbed the cream chiffon curtain between her fangs and pulled. She talked through the corner of her mouth. *Remember where they were so we can put them back for the humans.*

Duncan grabbed the other section of curtains and did as he was told. He lowered his voice to a whisper instinctively. *Who are you afraid of?*

Whiski twitched her stub tail. *Just a precaution. This is risky behavior. Another cat could spot us or report us. Computers leave a great deal of evidence. If we're not careful, the humans could catch on, or worse.*

132

What do you mean, or worse?

Whiski sighed. *There are cats out there who believe mixed-breeds must be "monitored" in their interaction with humans. If you break the rules and they catch you... well, let's put it this way... you don't want them to catch you.*

Duncan swallowed hard. *Do you know if any cats like that live around here?*

Whiski looked back at Duncan. *For being an all-powerful Son of Sagira, you're acting like such a pussycat. That's why we closed the curtains. And no, I have no idea if there are cats like that in our neighborhood, but our fat Persian friend, Franklin, sure talks like he's one, so I'm not gonna take any chances!*

Duncan stood wide-eyed and very still.

Well, Whiski huffed, *Are you ready?*

Duncan's voice cracked. *Yeah, yeah, let's do this.* He was trying to control the anxiety that was shooting throughout his body. Someone could have seen him use his powers. After all, he couldn't control or predict them. The power of sight, that could be hidden, but fire, someone would certainly notice if he went up in flames.

Whiski tapped her claws on the plywood desk. *Have you been listening to anything I've said?*

What? Duncan snapped out of his thoughts.

I was telling you what to do if the humans come back.

Oh yeah, I, uh... Duncan tried to look as if he was concentrating very hard.

In one swift motion, Whiski grabbed his whiskers with both of her paws and pulled his face close. *You are to stop what you are doing and start rolling around on the keyboard. Start pressing random buttons, so it looks like you turned on the computer by accident.*

Ouch! Okay, okay! Let go of my whiskers!

Whiski narrowed her eyes. Duncan massaged his muzzle tenderly.

She gestured with her stub tail. *Push the button.*

What button?

The power button. It has the same symbol as the TV power button.

Duncan let his paw run over the plastic box. *Okay,* he pushed the button until it glowed blue. *Got it!*

Come up here, then.

Duncan leapt up to join Whiski on the desk.

Okay, Whiski pushed what looked like a glowing plastic ball on the desk. She let out a dry laugh. *Can you believe they call this thing a mouse?*

The screen lit up.

Duncan let his paw touch the glowing surface. Whiski slapped it down.

No touching! You'll leave prints.

Duncan grumbled under his breath at Whiski.

A text box flashed on the screen.

What does it want? he asked.

A password. See, I told you this was dangerous. We'll have to make sure we log out at the end.

But we don't know the password!

Whiski smirked. *Watch and learn, Dunkelberry, watch and learn.*

Whiski stroked her whiskers as she thought through the human symbols for each letter. *The human woman is very predictable. She always uses some form of our names as her passwords. Then she says them out loud as she types them.* Whiski laughed. *Good thing she's never had to fend for herself. I don't think she'd survive very long in the wild.*

Duncan smiled. *Then again, she does know how to use a can opener and we don't.*

Yeah well, Whiski spoke mostly to herself, *there aren't a lot of cans in the wild, kid.*

With a final stroke of a key, the screen filled up with icons.

Duncan flicked his tail with excitement. *Whoa...*

Whiski wiggled the mouse until it hovered over the search engine icon and clicked.

She raised an eyebrow at Duncan. *Time to find your mommy, Son of Sagira.*

~

There are seven different Luthers in this area! How do we know which one to go to?

Whiski's eyebrow whiskers were furrowed in thought. *Do you remember anything else. A street name? A first name? Anything?*

135

Duncan sighed heavily. *No.*

What about if we used the satellite map from above? Would you be able to recognize it from the top?

Duncan's hopes were raised for a second and then came crashing down.

No, probably not. I never went outside. Only my mother was allowed outside, and she never let us come with her.

Whiski moved to log off the computer.

No, wait! There has to be something we can do!

Duncan, it's too risky to stay on the computer. We have to sign off now.

Duncan kicked the pencil holder over in frustration.

Hey! Watch it, kid!

Sorry, Duncan frowned. He was sulking, and he knew it.

Whiski growled in annoyance. *Stop acting like a moody teenager! I don't care if you can see the future or if you can burst into flames. I don't need you destroying things and sulking in dark corners on top of everything else. Act like a tomcat, and deal with it!*

Duncan nodded grudgingly to show that he understood Whiski's point, but he felt like disappearing. Everything seemed so hopeless. Maybe it would be better if let himself get lost in the shadows.

Duncan?

Duncan raised his head to look at Whiski. Her voice sounded panicked.

What?

Where are you?

Here, why?

Whiski leapt back, looking all around her. *I can't see you.*

What do you mean?

I mean, I... can't... see... you! Whiski gestured to her big green eyes like Duncan was stupid.

Duncan raised his paw and nearly lost his breakfast when he realized there was only air where his paw should have been.

No, no, no, no, no, no! This can't be happening! Duncan started running around the room in a panic.

Stop moving! Whiski yelled. *Stay still!*

Duncan slowed to a halt. His nose was starting to go numb. He was hyperventilating.

Why am I invisible?

You're asking me that?

Yeah! I sure have no idea!

Whiski was breathing quickly, but Duncan thought that this seemed to faze her less than the fire or the bacon incidents. Maybe she was getting used to him going through these changes, but he wasn't!

Whiski stopped. *How did the old kitten nursery rhyme go?*

What? Have you lost your mind?

Whiski held up her paw to silence him and closed her eyes.

Five from one

Three daughters and two sons

One with fire

One with sight

One to tell you wrong from right

One to hide

One to run

Each with the golden power of the sun

Duncan, Whiski cleared her throat, trying to sound calm and failing, *Duncan, you have the fourth power. You can become invisible.*

Duncan felt tears of anger pressing against his eyes. He said through clenched teeth. *How do I become visible again?*

I have no idea! How did you become invisible in the first place?

I don't know. I was thinking about how everything felt hopeless, and that I wished that I could just disappear, and...

Well, there's your answer. Whiski interrupted. *You wanted to become invisible, right? So ask to become visible again.*

There's no way it's going to be that easy, said Duncan doubtfully.

Just do it! Lord, you're whiney today!

Fine! Duncan growled.

Duncan let himself focus on the desire to become part of the world around him again, the desire to live and to be seen.

He opened his eyes and gazed down at his paws. He wiggled them to make sure he was seeing everything correctly.

Duncan lay down immediately. He was exhausted. He wasn't sure how much longer his body could keep up with all these changes.

Whiski looked disturbed but smug. *Next time I'd appreciate a little less lip from you.*

Duncan waved his tail in surrender and then let himself fall into the darkness of sleep.

Chapter 18

Whiski cursed silently to herself. Duncan had rallied for dinner but then had immediately fallen back asleep. The human couple had turned in for the night as well, so now it was just Whiski left awake and listening to the gentle sound of snoring mixed with the occasional passing car.

Duncan was lying belly-up with his legs splayed out and one paw over his head. His right foot kept flickering in and out of sight. Whiski threw a blanket over his legs and grumbled something about him not setting it on fire.

With a grunt, she leapt down from the bed and walked stiffly into the office. It was streaked with patches of moonlight, and she found an acceptable stretch of carpet to lie down on and think.

Whiski looked at her white-booted paws and let them sink into the soft carpet. They looked almost silver in the moonlight. She turned one of her paws over to look at scars left from walking on hard concrete and sharp summer grass.

Duncan was certainly trouble, big trouble. There was no doubt of that, but Whiski had a hard time believing that he would ever purposefully hurt her or the human couple. Then again, he didn't have to want to hurt them to end up hurting them. Whiski took a deep breath and let it out slowly. All she had to go on regarding the Children of Sagira were kitten rhymes and stories told to her when she was young. Whiski shook her head. Everything her mother had told her had made her picture something terrifying, godlike, and corrupt... nothing like what lay sleeping in the next room.

Instead, this Son of Sagira was in the form of a gangly teenager who sporadically disappeared and burst into flames. Who would have ever thought she'd actually meet one of Sagira's descendants. And not just one of them. No, Duncan was a mystery even among the mysterious. Go figure. She had remembered asking her mother why the Children of Sagira were so hated. Her mother had replied, *Because they deserved it.*

Whiski lowered her head to rest on her paws. She had believed her mother then, now she wasn't so sure. She let her eyes close. There were decisions to be made, and the way Whiski figured it, she really only had two choices. 1. Help Duncan find his mother, wherever that path lead the two of them, or 2. Send Duncan off to find his mother alone, knowing that he probably wouldn't survive one night alone outside. Could she live with herself if she did that? After all, Duncan had agreed that she didn't have to go with him. He couldn't blame her if she chose to stay. Besides, what did she owe him? Not a darned thing, she thought to herself. This was his search, and even if she did go with him, it didn't guarantee that they'd find his mother or that she'd have any answers.

It was safer to stay. It was smarter to stay.

Whiski opened her green eyes and stared out into the night. She wished she could talk to her brother. She could sure use his advice right now.

She swore that some nights she could feel him sitting next to her in the moonlight. Tonight was one of those nights. It was a nice thought, even if it made her feel crazy for thinking it, and even if it was just an empty patch of moonlight.

What do you think? Should I help him? She felt her throat tighten with emotion. *You'd like him, you know. He's a total freak, of course, but you'd like him.*

Whiski paused and closed her eyes. She knew what her decision was. She turned her head toward the empty strip of moonlight on the carpet. *I'm about to do something incredibly stupid. I don't know if you can hear me but, if you can, please keep an eye out for us, okay? Your little sister has her paws full.*

She raised herself up slowly and walked back to the bedroom.

All three of them were still asleep. Duncan had kicked the blanket off and was now snoring along with the human man. There was an empty shadow where his foot should have been. Whiski pulled the blanket back over Duncan and then laid her head on his stomach. He was warm to the touch.

~

Both cats awoke to the bright lights of a camera flash. The human woman held a camera over them.

"Oh, no! I woke them up! Stay right there, you're so cute right now!" The camera flashed again.

Duncan growled and stuffed his head under the blanket, and Whiski

142

turned so that her butt was the only thing facing the camera.

"Oh, shoot." The woman looked sad, but then gave up quickly after she realized both cats had given her a firm, nonverbal, *No!*

Duncan rubbed his temples. He felt like he'd slept for days. Whiski yawned and stretched and quickly moved herself away from Duncan.

Duncan's voice was still groggy. *Did you figure anything out after I fell asleep?*

Food first, muttered Whiski sleepily, *then we'll talk.*

Duncan shrugged in agreement and both cats padded into the kitchen.

Duncan looked out of the window and nearly choked on his meaty mush. *Franklin looks like he's about to fall out of that tree.*

Whiski followed Duncan's gaze and a huge grin broke across her face. *It would appear that Franklin fell asleep in the middle of stalking something.*

Should we wake him up? Duncan asked in an amused voice.

Nah, mumbled Whiski through mouthfuls of mush.

Both cats ate quietly and tried to keep from falling over laughing when they heard a thud and a yowl outside their backyard. Well, Franklin was awake now.

Duncan peeked around the window and waved at a very flustered Franklin. Franklin's eyes got huge as soon as he saw Duncan waving at him. He took off running as fast as his fat orange legs could carry him.

Duncan looked over at Whiski. *That was odd.*

She shrugged. *That's Franklin.*

Chapter 19

The humans were making quite a ruckus in the bedroom, and Duncan and Whiski had yet to talk about how they were going to find out which Luther house was the one where he was born.

Whiski stopped in the doorframe of the bedroom and pretended to casually groom herself while she whispered to Duncan (who looked wide-eyed and confused).

They're packing.

Why? Where are they going? he whispered back.

Don't know, but they've got their big suitcase out. Try to figure out how many shirts she's got in there.

The woman was folding clothes and placing them in a large red suitcase while the man collected various human bathing products from the bathroom.

Duncan leapt up on the bed and was just about to plop down on a stack of sweaters in order to count them when the woman picked him up.

Whiski rolled her eyes.

The human woman kissed Duncan's head.

"Don't worry, Dunkelberry! We'll only be gone four days, and we're not leaving until this afternoon." She scratched Whiski's head. "We'll make sure you guys have more than enough food and water and a nice, fresh litter box!"

Whiski gestured at Duncan when the woman's back was turned. She whispered. *If we're going to find your mom, we need to start tonight while they're gone. It's our best chance.*

Duncan blinked in disbelief. *We?*

Whiski shushed Duncan while the man walked by. *Don't make me change my mind.*

Duncan grinned and tackled Whiski in a gigantic bear hug.

Whiski hissed and popped Duncan on the nose. *No hugging!* She patted down her fur in disgust while Duncan rubbed his nose. He was still smiling.

Whiski lowered her voice to a hiss. *Don't get too excited. We still don't know which family it is or where they live.*

Duncan felt a twinge in his gut. He had an idea, but Whiski wouldn't like it. He was sure that would be the case because he didn't even like it.

What? Whiski looked questioningly at Duncan. *What are you thinking?*

You're not going to like it.

Whiski scowled. *Why? What is it?*

Duncan lowered his voice. *If I ask...* he didn't even want to finish the idea out loud... *If I ask the woman to tell me, she'll tell me.*

Whiski's eyes got huge. Duncan read fear and concern in them. *Will it hurt her? You can't hurt her.* She looked almost pleadingly at Duncan, and it made him uncomfortable. He wasn't used to that kind of reaction from her.

He placed his paw over her paw, and it covered hers completely. *I would never hurt them, or you, but I don't know what other choice I have. If I continue like this, I'll end up hurting all of you, whether or not I want to. I need to find my mother, and to do that, we need that address.*

Whiski looked at the woman still packing her clothes. She nodded reluctantly.

Duncan began to walk toward the woman, and then without warning, the she called out to her husband.

"We should send the picture of Duncan and Whiski to the Luthers."

"What?" The man yelled back.

"You know," the woman sounded annoyed with her husband, "David and Laura Luther! Over in Watercress Village. They'll want to know how he's doing."

~

Hours passed, and after much hugging and kissing, the humans finally said goodbye to both cats. Almost immediately after the deadbolt locked, Duncan started racing toward the kitchen. He pulled open the cabinet where the Ziploc bags were kept, grabbed one, and ran toward their bowls of kibble.

Whiski grabbed him by the tail, causing Duncan to drop the bag and yowl in surprise.

What are you doing?

I'm packing! What do you think I'm doing?

You really were planning on carrying a Ziploc bag of kibble with you?

Duncan nodded. *What else would we have to eat?*

Whiski stared blankly at him.

What? I could hang it around my neck or strap it to my back. I've seen the rescue dogs do it on TV.

Whiski shook her head. *Put the bag down and follow me. We need to find these people and memorize the directions.*

Duncan scowled but did as he was told.

Whiski examined the room. *Good thing the humans shut the curtains for us. One less thing we have to take care of.*

Whiski turned on the computer, wiggled the mouse, and entered the password. Duncan was amazed at Whiski's speed on the computer. Within 10 minutes, she had mapped their route to Duncan's first home.

Whiski heaved a heavy sigh. *It's 3 miles away. That's doable, and I guess we should be glad that it's as close as it is, but it's still going to be a long trip. Several hours at least, at a fast pace too if we want to make it back by dawn.*

Duncan couldn't help it. He was terrified but exhilarated at the same time. *Now what do we do?*

Whiski powered down the computer and thought carefully. *Eat as much food and drink as much water as you can. We'll leave in three hours.* Whiski eyed the clock. *Traffic will have died down, and it'll be good and dark. We'll cover our white spots with dust from the fireplace. We want to attract as little attention as possible.*

Duncan nodded.

Oh, and Duncan?

Yeah?

Sharpen your claws.

~

Time passed slowly for both cats, but darkness finally arrived, and it was as safe as it would ever be to begin their journey.

Both cats stood by the back window. Whiski pushed up on the lock, but before she slid open the window, she stopped. *Duncan, I need you to promise me something.*

Duncan nodded, *Yeah, anything.*

Look me in the eyes and promise me you won't use your powers on me.

Duncan's gold eyes shimmered against the darkness of the night. He stopped and looked directly at Whiski. He could see the shape of her eyes, but he couldn't read her expression.

Whiski, you have my word and my protection.

He could hear Whiski's dry laugh.

We'll see who ends up protecting who, Dunkelberry.

PART THREE

Chapter 20

With a click, Whiski slid open the window. She carefully pushed out on the corner of the thin screen separating them from the outside world. Duncan braced himself as a cold gust of air whipped through his fur. He gasped and his claws retracted. Tucking his tail down, he whispered to himself, *Wow, that's cold.*

Whiski huffed. *They don't keep it at 70 degrees out here, Dunkelberry.* She pushed the window back so that it was barely open. She lowered her voice. *This crack should be just enough to slip our claws in and pull when we get back.*

I just, Duncan reluctantly let his lungs fill with cold air. *I just wasn't ready.*

Whiski looked out into the night. Her voice was serious. *You ready now?*

Duncan looked at Whiski and nodded. He leapt to the ground. The snow had melted, but the grass was still wet and cold. He'd never felt anything but carpet or tile against his paw pads. Without any action on his part, Duncan's body began to generate heat. Not fire this time, but heat. Duncan could feel the earth warming under his paws. He whispered. *That's odd...*

Whiski checked the window several times and then leapt down beside him. *What's odd?* He watched her shiver against a strong gust of wind. Duncan started to move to help warm her and then stopped himself. He shook his head. *Nothing. I'm ready now.*

A familiar voice came from behind them. *Ready for what, exactly?*

Whiski unsheathed her claws, and with one swift lunge, she had turned and pinned Franklin against the fence.

Franklin snarled and hissed. *Take your paws off me! I've done nothing wrong!* He growled, baring his long fangs.

Duncan laid his paw on Whiski's and motioned for her to let go. The last thing they needed was Franklin suspicious, though perhaps it was too late for that. She eyed Duncan skeptically and removed her grip on Franklin's throat.

Franklin straightened his fur, and then, without warning he swung his massive orange paw against Whiski's muzzle, knocking her to the ground. *I'll expect better manners from you next time.*

Duncan growled and tackled Franklin and held him furiously against the ground.

You are not allowed to touch my family!

Franklin was no match for Duncan, who could barely control his anger. What had started as a slow burn inside Duncan had grown into something that could easily engulf them both.

Struggling to control his rage, Duncan hissed. *Why are you here?*

Out for my evening walk! Franklin struggled, but it was no use.

Whiski had been watching Franklin angrily. She rubbed her sore cheek. *He's lying.*

Franklin whipped his head around to look at Whiski. *How dare you accuse me? What were you two doing out?* Franklin thrashed against Duncan's hold, still to no avail. *You're indoor cats... you're not supposed to be out here! What are you up to? Where are your humans?*

Duncan knew he was beginning to burn Franklin, but he tightened his hold. His eyes were glowing brighter now. They needed to move quickly. He moved one of his paws onto Franklin's throat and pressed down.

Franklin, Duncan hissed in almost a whisper, *Look at me.* Franklin's eyes began to flutter. He was suddenly still. Duncan continued, *Why are you here?*

Franklin looked at Duncan and blinked several times. His watery yellow eyes never left Duncan's golden ones. *I'm on guard. I'm here to watch you. I've been ordered to watch you.*

Whiski shot Duncan a troubled look. She brought her face within an inch of Franklin's and hissed. *Who sent you?*

Franklin blinked vacantly at Duncan. He didn't even look at Whiski.

Who ordered you, Franklin? whispered Duncan.

V...Vera?

Skillfully, a chocolate-brown Persian tackled Whiski from behind. She held her sharpened claws a whiskers' width from Whiski's green eyes. *Let go of my brother, mixed-breed, or your friend shall find herself with one less eye!*

Whiski muttered through clenched teeth, *That's funny. I didn't think Persians knew how to fight.*

Silence! I shall remove both of your insolent eyes for this! But in her anger Vera had changed her grip just enough that with one thrust of her paw, Whiski jabbed the brown Persian in the ribs, rotated her body clockwise beneath Vera's and threw the chocolate Persian onto her back.

Whiski smiled. *Oh right, that's because you don't.*

A porch light snapped on two houses down.

Whiski tilted her head toward Duncan. *We need to get out of here. We can't leave them like this. They know far more than they should. They won't leave us alone if they think we've violated one of the laws. They're part of the guard.*

You should be thankful, you disgraceful beasts! Vera hissed. *We keep the balance! You are no longer in the Dark Times because of us. We enforce the rules with the humans. We do this to protect you, to protect all of us!*

Whiski pushed down on Vera's throat.

Duncan's voice had an edge of panic. He was losing Franklin. *What should we do?*

I command you to release us! snapped Vera. *Varik will determine your punishment!*

Ignoring Vera, Whiski raised her eyebrow whiskers knowingly at

Duncan. *Can't you do something special?*

Duncan raised his eyebrows back. *Like?*

Whiski narrowed her eyes, blinked hard, and used her stub tail to emphasize her gesture. *You know... one of your special talents?*

Franklin was almost out of Duncan's influence. They didn't have a numbers advantage anymore, and they couldn't hold them all night. His power of persuasion wouldn't work. It would wear off too quickly, especially if they were already being watched. They needed more time to escape. Besides, he wasn't even sure it would work on more than one cat at a time. Despite the heat building within him, Duncan felt a shiver run down his spine. He needed to blind them. Duncan stared down at Franklin. It was dangerous. His mother had warned him of using their power on someone who wasn't a Child of Sagira. But she had also told him to use it in an emergency. Duncan looked over at Whiski who was beginning to have difficulty holding onto Vera, who was roughly twice her size. If this didn't qualify as an emergency, Duncan wasn't sure what did.

Any of your special talents! said Whiski more urgently.

Look at me. Duncan moved his eyes within an inch of Franklin's. Franklin's eyes widened and then went dull. He went completely limp.

Vera began to yowl. Even Whiski looked unnerved by what had just taken place.

What have you done to him? Vera yelled, her eyes widening with fear as she put the pieces together.

Duncan moved toward Vera as Whiski held her. *Stay away from me,*

157

you freak! Vera struggled against Whiski's hold. *Varik will punish you for this! You'll get what you deserve! Both of you!*

Look at me. Duncan's eyes pulsed, and then there was silence.

Whiski let go and stepped back. She looked exhausted.

Did you just do what I think you did?

Duncan fought his own memories of darkness mixed with nausea. He nodded. He hadn't planned for the night to start like this. He cleared his throat, trying to sound confident. *They'll wake up sometime tomorrow. I've never done this before... well, other than practicing with my mom. She said to use it in an emergency...* Duncan's voice kept trailing off as he spoke each thought.

Whiski shook her head. *And we haven't even left the yard yet...*

Duncan gave Whiski a tired smile. Whiski kept her face serious, but Duncan could tell she was proud of herself. She looked down and frowned. *We need to move them.*

Duncan nodded and looked down at Franklin.

You get Frankilin, Whiski gestured, *and I'll get the girl.*

Whiski muttered under her breath. *I feel like mafia cats...*

It took almost a half an hour, with extensive breaks, but they had managed to drag both Franklin and Vera to Franklin's back porch. They shoved both cats through Franklin's human's cat door and arranged them so that they looked like they had fallen asleep cuddled together.

Duncan sighed and rubbed his jaw. Too bad he didn't get any super strength. He wasn't prepared to carry a 20-pound Persian.

And you're sure they won't remember? Whiski looked down at the two motionless bodies.

Duncan nodded, though in truth, he wasn't entirely sure.

Whiski shook her head in shock. *I had heard that the power of sight could be used to blind other cats, but I'd never imagined that I would see it done.* She turned to look at Duncan. *I don't know what to believe anymore.*

Duncan let them sit in silence for a little while. *Believe that I'm your friend.*

Whiski looked sadly at Duncan and patted him on the shoulder. She looked around to orient herself and then began walking. Duncan followed quickly behind her.

Neither cat said a word for the first hour of their journey.

Chapter 21

They stayed away from the streets and kept to the shadows as much as possible. Duncan could see very little in the night except for the long stretches of hedges, fences, and neighborhood trees that loomed over them. Whiski kept them moving at a fast pace, slowing only to verify landmarks and sometimes to identify strange noises in the dark. Duncan finally broke their uncomfortable silence. *Are we close?* He was breathing heavily. He wasn't used to running long distances.

Probably another hour. We need to keep moving. Why, you need a break?

No, well, sort of. I'm bored.

Whiski's voice was annoyed. *You should be glad it's boring, Dunkelberry. I'm doing my best to make sure it's boring.*

Duncan yawned and then stopped when he saw Whiski glare at him over her shoulder.

So tell me how you know all this outdoorsy-survival stuff?

What do you mean? We're in the suburbs, Duncan.

Duncan gestured into the surrounding night with his tail. *You know what I mean... surviving outside, how to not be seen, how to find your way around... how did you learn all this cool stuff?*

Whiski sighed. *Sometimes in life you learn things because you have to. I learned all this stuff because I had to.* She slowed her pace. *I lived outside with my brother. We'd been abandoned when our first family moved. They left us...* Whiski cleared her throat.

Duncan felt a surge of guilt. He'd spent so much time feeling sorry for himself lately. *On purpose?* he asked hesitantly.

He could see Whiski's breath in the night. *Yeah, on purpose.*

Duncan shook his head. He couldn't imagine their young couple abandoning them. *Are there lots of humans like that?* Duncan asked, moving quickly to keep pace with Whiski.

Whiski huffed. *Far too many.* Then she spoke softly. *But then you have nice ones.*

Duncan nodded thoughtfully. *The kind who give deli-meat scraps.*

Whiski chuckled under her breath, and they continued on quietly.

She paused to point out a fenced yard to their right. *You hear that?*

Hear what? he whispered.

Shhh... she covered his mouth with her paw. Duncan made a face as she got mud and grass all over his muzzle. *Listen,* she whispered.

At first Duncan heard nothing, then all of a sudden he noticed it: The sound of claws clicking on a cement porch. Duncan's ears went back in alarm.

She mouthed one word, *Raccoons,* and then continued to move forward.

Once they were a safe distance away, she spoke again. *You don't want to mess with a pack of wild raccoons. Trust me. Each one is bigger than both of us combined, and they're always in the mood to fight.*

Duncan looked over his shoulder and whispered to Whiski. *Are you sure they're not following us?*

Yeah, kid. I'm just trying to teach you how to survive out here. Whiski pointed behind them with her tail stub. *Raccoons equal bad, got it?*

Duncan couldn't help but smirk into the darkness. *Yeah, got it.*

Whiski continued. *Raccoons are nasty, filthy beasts, but they're stupid. If you learn how to spot them and keep your distance, you'll be okay. They purr though, so you gotta make sure you don't mistake them for cats.*

Whiski kept them moving at a fast pace, but she made sure to point out features of the land to Duncan, should they ever get separated. Duncan took the information willingly, but there was no way he was letting Whiski out of his sight. He was feeling less and less confident about his ability to survive on his own, even if they were just in the suburbs.

Whiski stopped again. *Do you hear that?* Duncan's ears flicked forward. It was the faintest of scratches, but he could hear it. He nodded. Whiski smiled and mouthed the word. *Mouse.*

Duncan's tail began to flick excitedly. He'd never chased a real mouse before.

Whiski gestured with her tail for them to keep moving. She whispered. *If we had more time, I'd teach you how to catch one.*

Duncan puffed out his chest. *I think I could manage.*

Whiski snorted. *Kid, these mice aren't stuffed and rainbow colored. They run fast and they fight back.*

Duncan frowned. *Wait, is that what you* ate?

Whiski shrugged. *Well, mice and birds when we could catch 'em. Garbage scraps when we couldn't....*

Duncan wrinkled his nose thinking about it. *How long did you have to live out in the wild?*

Six months.

What happened after six months?

Whiski stopped and then continued. *I let the animal cops find me. They took me to the shelter. I thought they were going to kill me, but they cleaned me up and fed me. I bounced from home to home for a while...* she rolled her eyes at Duncan, *trying to avoid all the stupid kittens in foster care.*

Duncan looked quizzically at Whiski. She was hiding something behind her humor. She always did.

Why did you let them find you?

Whiski was quiet.

Duncan tried again. *Why would you do that if you thought they were going to kill you?*

Whiski's voice went cold. *My brother was dead. I wanted to die, too.*

Duncan stopped in his tracks, but began walking again when he realized Whiski wasn't going to stop. He wanted to know what happened to her brother, but he didn't have the heart to ask.

Life doesn't always move in ways we can predict, Dunkelberry.

More time passed between the two cats.

I'm really sorry, Whiski.

Not your fault, Dunkelberry.

Besides, Whiski let out a sigh, *now I'm out here helping you on your quest for knowledge, not to mention I've had the pleasure of beating up two purebreds in the process.*

Duncan gave Whiski a perplexed look. *Yay?*

Whiski winked, *Yay, indeed.*

Duncan smiled back and continued walking. *What did you know about the Children of Sagira before you met me?*

Whiski's smile faded. *Nothing very nice. Let's leave it at that.*

They walked the next few blocks in silence.

This mother of yours... Does she know we're coming?

Duncan shook his head anxiously. *I'm not sure. I had the vision, but I don't know if she did.*

Whiski stopped suddenly and held up her paw for Duncan to stop as well. He walked into her paw and then looked up at what made her stop.

It was his first home. They had found it.

Chapter 22

Now what?

What do you mean?

I got you here. Now what's your plan to get in?

Duncan gulped. He hadn't really figured that part out yet.

Can't you signal her with your brain or something?

Duncan glared at Whiski.

So I take it you can't do that? Whiski smirked then shrugged her shoulders. *There are lots of rumors about your kind, kid.*

Duncan sat down. His paws were killing him. They weren't used to this kind of terrain, or any terrain other than fluffy carpet and hardwood floors.

Well...?

Shhh, I'm thinking, Duncan gave Whiski an irritated look.

Whiski rolled her eyes.

Wait, I know where she is! Duncan motioned for Whiski to follow him around to the back of the house. They approached the sliding-glass door slowly. Duncan sat down and looked in through the door. It was strange to be sitting on the other side of the glass. He looked longingly inside the room and then shook his head. That was another life. No sign of his sisters or his mother.

What now? whispered Whiski.

Duncan signaled for her to be quiet. He whispered. *She always spent the night on guard. She'll see us.* Without warning, a pair of golden eyes identical to Duncan's appeared on the other side of the glass. They were angry.

~

Whiski backed up a few steps. *Looks like your mom found us.*

Duncan tried to give his mom a small smile. Surely she would have seen him coming.

Duncan wasn't fully grown yet, but he was almost Nellie's height. Standing face to face with just the glass between them, Nellie gestured for them to wait over by a small collection of bushes in the backyard. She was coming outside.

Whiski patted Duncan on the haunches to get him moving. He walked slowly, still stunned by his mother's reaction.

I thought she would be happy to see me, Duncan spoke the words aloud to himself.

Maybe she is, answered Whiski. *Mothers are capable of feeling thousands of different emotions about their children, all at the same time. I'm sure "happy" is buried in there somewhere.*

Duncan shot Whiski a worried look and stopped in his tracks.

Whiski nudged him forward a few more steps. *Time to talk turkey, Dunkelberry. Come on. The clock is ticking.*

Nellie appeared noiselessly from the other side of the bushes, her movement as smooth and black as the shadows.

Why have you come back, Duncan?

Nice to see you, too, muttered Duncan.

Nellie sighed. *You know that it makes me happy to see you, but it also makes me very afraid for you as well. Why have you come here? Why have you brought this stranger with you?*

Whiski hissed in offense.

This isn't a stranger, Mom. Whiski is my friend.

Nellie looked at Whiski then back to her son. Her face was hard.

She's not your friend, Duncan.

Whiski began to stiffen in anger. *Little harsh there, aren't we, Mom? I did bring him all the way here to see you.*

Nellie scowled at Whiski. *Then I have you to blame.* She addressed her son. *Duncan, you know friends are a luxury you can't have.*

No, Mom, she knows who I am! She knows everything! She's my friend!

Nellie's eyes widened. Whatever she expected Duncan to say, it was not that. She moved forward grabbed his muzzle in her paws. *This can't continue, Duncan! It isn't safe! How could you be so reckless?* Nellie turned toward Whiski, her eyes ready to pulse. Whiski unsheathed her claws and positioned herself for a fight against the much larger queen.

Duncan stepped between the two. *Mom, no! You aren't allowed to blind her. She is under my protection.*

Nellie didn't move a muscle except to raise one eyebrow. *She's under your "protection"?*

Whiski sighed, *I know, right?*

Duncan raised his chin in defiance. *Yes, she is my friend and my family, and I promised her I would protect her,* his voice shook slightly, *even from you, Mom.*

The three of them stood there, deadlocked. Nellie staring at Whiski, Whiski staring at Nellie, and Duncan nervously looking back and forth between them.

Nellie finally let her eyes leave Whiski and settle back on her son. Her eyes were burning bright gold with anger and fear. *Why are you here?*

Duncan felt himself exhale. He hadn't realized he'd been holding his breath. *Didn't you see me coming?*

Nellie looked surprised by his question. *Yes, and I was furious you would do something so risky! What if someone followed you? What if your sisters saw you?*

Duncan raised a paw to interrupt her. *How are my sisters?*

Nellie's body relaxed slightly. *They are well. They miss you, but they are well.*

Duncan's eyes were full of concern thinking about the last time he had seen them. *And Anna?*

Nellie spoke cautiously in front of Whiski. *Anna is well.*

Duncan exhaled in relief. *Good.*

They sat in silence for a few minutes. Whiski watched them uncomfortably from a few feet back but said nothing.

Duncan finally spoke. *Mom, did you see why I came to you?*

Nellie frowned. *No, that was hidden from me.*

Mom, I need your help.

Nellie narrowed her eyes and looked at Whiski. *Your "friend" cannot help you?*

Whiski grumbled under her breath. *I already have, lady.*

Duncan continued. He hadn't realized how much it meant to him to share this with his mother. *I'm changing, Mom.* He reached out his paw to touch hers, and the heat made Nellie pull her paw back in surprise.

What is this?

Whiski gestured at Duncan, *There's more where that came from.*

Duncan shot Whiski a look to let her know she wasn't helping.

Whiski rolled her eyes but stayed silent.

Nellie swallowed hard. *Tell her to leave.*

Duncan began to protest.

I will not speak of these things in front of her.

Duncan looked pleadingly at Whiski, and just as she had in the vision, she rolled her eyes, cursed, and stomped off to wait for Duncan by the side of the house.

Nellie waited for Whiski to pass out of sight before she finally spoke.

Duncan, this is not possible. No one has ever held more than one of Sagira's powers. For you to hold two...

Duncan swished his tail in frustration. *Are you sure no one else has held more than one?*

Nellie stammered. *It is legend... it has been passed down for hundreds of years. None since Sagira...*

As Nellie spoke, Duncan's tail flicked out of view and reappeared seconds later.

Nellie sat down on the cold ground. She couldn't believe this. This shouldn't be happening. Her chest was heaving. *Three powers!*

Mom, Duncan's voice was steadier now. *Mom, I have four of the five powers.*

Nellie shook her head. *No... no. This is not possible. You have the power of sight...*

Yes, and I have the power of fire, invisibility, and persuasion.

Nellie shook her head, stunned.

Mom, are you sure my father didn't have any powers?

171

No, of course not. Nellie said in a tired voice. *Your father was...* Nellie paused, *not like us.*

Then how...?

I do not know! Nellie snapped. *Our kind cannot breed with each other, even if we wanted to, we can only bear children with cats who are not descendants of Sagira.*

Duncan puffed out his fur in frustration. *Then what am I?*

You are beyond me. Nellie kept shaking her head. *I have never even met another with the power of sight, save my mother, much less any of the other powers. We do not reveal ourselves, not even to one another. That is why it was so dangerous for you to come here. It is dangerous for our kind to associate at all.*

Then what do I do? Duncan's voice had a growing panic to it. *I thought you would be able to help me learn how to control it! How am I supposed to live like this?*

Nellie stared with sad, scared eyes at her son. She didn't want to cause him more pain, but her son's frantic face fell on her with such intensity she spoke what she knew to be true.

You must run away, Duncan. If you are truly like Sagira, I have no help to give you. I do not know how to control these other powers.

But my family? No!

It is the only way to keep them safe, Duncan. You must come to terms with that as well. I know this isn't what you wanted to hear...

Duncan's voice hardened. *So you're telling me, there is no information anywhere about the Children of Sagira and their powers? I'm just supposed to give up?* He spoke the words sharply.

A single tear fell from Nellie's sun-colored eye. Duncan had never seen his mother cry. Not when she'd had to blind him, not when she'd had to say goodbye to him...

Am I that lost to you, Mom? Tears for your doomed son! Duncan's voice was shaking. *I don't believe that there's no one out there who can help me! There has to be someone who knows something!*

Nellie shook her head. *There are only myths and legends about our kind, Duncan. There were only two groups who witnessed the rise and fall of Sagira and her Children; the purebreds and the ferals. The mixed-breeds... they know very little beyond the nursery rhymes told to them as kittens.* She paused, exasperated. *The ferals valued, above all things, custom and history. While the purebreds tried to destroy all things connected with our kind, the ferals tried to save it. It is said the ferals kept writings of Sagira and her Children, though I do not know if this is true. Something of such value as the writings of Sagira, if they still exist, would be deeply hidden and protected.*

Well then, how can I find them? asked Duncan intently. *Would they be able to help me?*

Nellie stared off into the distance, not wishing to let her eyes meet with her son's. *That is the problem, Duncan. The ferals were hunted along with the Sons and Daughters of Sagira. What ferals are left or where they live, I do not know. They are almost impossible to find, as many of them live in the wild or underground. They are suspicious, secretive creatures. Even if you found one of them, they would die before they told you anything. Just as I told you when you were young, hate lives on long after love dies. There is much deceit that surrounds our kind,*

Duncan, and most of it is our own doing.

Duncan inhaled slowly and painfully. He could feel the heat increasing in his body even though it was getting colder outside.

Isn't there anything that could help me, Mom? Please?

Nellie put her paw on Duncan's. It was hot to the touch. She pulled it back.

Duncan looked away. Tears were burning in his eyes. He shook his head angrily. It was beginning to snow lightly. It was collecting on the ground and on Nellie's black fur. It gave her an ethereal white glow against the night. She spoke softly.

Duncan, you must get your friend home. And then... if you love her and if you love your human family, you must leave them. This power within you, it is too much. Nellie's voice broke with emotion. *In her time, Sagira was worshiped as a goddess, but in our time only terrible things could come from witnessing what you are capable of, and Duncan, you are capable of more than I ever thought possible. Trust me, you do not want to see your family pay the price for what you are. It would destroy you, Duncan, as it destroys me to have done this to you.*

Nellie moved forward to hold her son tightly in her arms even though it burned. *I love you, Duncan, and I am sorry.*

Duncan put his head on top of his mother's. When their bodies met, power surged through both of them like electricity. Flames ran down Duncan's tail, and his visibility flicked on and off like a dying light bulb. Their combined power was both wondrous and terrifying to behold, yet it was a sight seen by no one.

174

I love you, Mom. Duncan licked her head gently. *But I will not walk away from my family. I am not Sagira. I will not accept her fate.* He inhaled deeply into her fur one last time to try to breath in what was left of his childhood. He turned to walk back toward Whiski.

As he walked, the flames slowly spread across his body until he was a torch against the night... the snow parting around him, melting before it hit the ground.

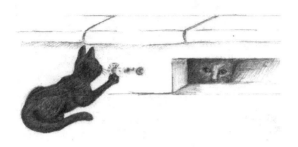

Chapter 23

Duncan, wait. Nellie's voice was shaking. *Duncan?*

Duncan stopped but he did not turn to face his mother. *Yes, Mom?*

I need you to look at me, just like when you were little. I need you to bring your eyes level with mine. Look at me.

Just as he had in the vision, Duncan hesitated. The flames covering his body went down, like someone turned the knob on a gas burner.

Nellie's voice softened. *Trust me.*

Duncan's shoulders dropped. He turned and let his golden eyes lock with hers.

What do you see?

~

Duncan's vision went black. Had she blinded him? No, this was definitely something else. All of a sudden, images began flashing out from the darkness. He could feel Nellie pulling him back. The images kept flipping, like pages in a book, until Nellie had found what she was looking for.

Duncan looked down at his paws. They were no longer his. From what he could tell, he was in a cold steel cage with a small cardboard litter box, a bowl of water, and a worn-out human bath towel. The sounds of yowling echoed around the room. He could smell the other cats, their food, their urine, but none of their faces were visible, except for the one across from him. It was a large female cat, calico, with wild green eyes. Her gaze made him uncomfortable.

Where are we? asked Duncan, but it was not Duncan's voice that spoke. It was a young female's voice, and it was scared. Duncan recognized it instantly as his mother's, but she was young, a kitten still.

The large calico didn't respond, but continued to stare intensely at Nellie as if trying to solve a puzzle while unknowingly sitting on one of the pieces.

When there was no response, the cat from the cage below answered in a tired voice. *The shelter, child, we're in the human shelter.*

Duncan could see his mother's paws shaking as she drew the bath towel around her.

Images started moving forward rapidly again. Duncan could tell time had elapsed, but he was still in the cage, and the large calico was still watching him intensely.

What's your name? spoke Nellie, grabbing the bars of the cage with her claws. *Why do you look at me that way?*

The calico smiled but said nothing.

Night fell, and Duncan was woken up by whispers. *Do you still wish to know who I am?* The calico spoke into the darkness. *I believe I now know who you are. I have been watching you.*

Nellie backed into the corner of her cage. *What do you mean?*

The calico just smiled. *Do not fear.* Her wild green eyes reflected in the night. *I am known to my clan as Lenira.*

Your clan? Listen, I don't know who you think I am, but...

Do you really not know? The calico asked curiously, tilting her head to stare at Nellie.

Nellie didn't speak but turned to face away from the intensity of the female cat's stare.

Don't be scared, whispered the large female. *I have spent my whole life devoted to your kind.*

Nellie was gripping the worn towel tightly but stayed quiet.

I do not think it was by chance that we have found each another. I believe I was meant to see you, and you me, though I fear my time left here in this world is short.

Nellie hissed under her breath. *You're crazy.*

Lenira lowered her voice. *I have been called that before, but at this moment, and after meeting you, I have never been so sure of my sanity.*

Nellie finally turned and moved forward. Her nose was pressed against the cold bars. *Who are you, really?*

The calico bowed. *I am Lenira, daughter of Paki, and queen of the feral clan of Haji. I protect the past from those who would seek to destroy it.*

Again, Duncan felt time spinning forward.

Nellie was older now, but not by much. He could see her paws moving quickly in the dark grass. She was outside his old house and moving south under the cover of night. Time passed and he could see his mother running her paw along marks in the concrete. They were subtle, but distinct if you looked closely. She followed the trail down into the gutter. Arms grabbed her. Claws were dangerously close to piercing her neck.

Why do you follow us?

I am a friend of Lenira! I seek the feral clan of Haji! Nellie gasped for breath.

Duncan flashed forward again. Nellie was in his old house. She was alone, staring out of the sliding-glass door. She looked down and Duncan could tell that her belly was swollen. She spoke to a tomcat with bright green eyes, outlined in black, sitting on the other side of the glass. *We are leaving,* he whispered. *You must not come looking for us. You must promise this.*

Nellie hit the glass with her tail in anger. *Can you walk away so easily?*

The tomcat lowered his voice to a hiss. *To have the Book and a Child of Sagira together,* the tomcat narrowed his green eyes, *Nellie, you know the risk that poses. The guard would stop at nothing! They would kill every last one of us! Your kind was not meant to walk this path.*

Nellie's voice rose. *My kind was meant to live and die alone! Is that what you mean?*

The tomcat smiled sadly. *You know that is not what I meant.* He spoke softly. *I could not bear to cause you any more pain than I already have. You are safer here.* He touched the glass tenderly with his paw. *Are there any in your belly who are like you?*

Nellie shook her head firmly. *I walk alone.*

Nellie, I...

Both cats heard a noise coming from the bushes. The tomcat looked one last time at Nellie. His voice was desperate. *Do not follow. It is not safe. They will come for you. Promise me.* He hissed. *Promise me, Nellie!*

Nellie lowered her head, but she did not speak. When she looked up again, he was gone.

~

Nellie let her hold on Duncan go, and fell exhausted to the ground. Duncan staggered and fought to regain his balance. He was breathing heavily. *I didn't know we could do that.*

Nellie nodded. *Yes, it was the way secrets of old were passed among our kind. In the way that we can blind others with our own visions, we can also share them with those we trust. Though it requires a great deal of control to do it without having the same effect as the blinding,* her voice was heavy. *The mixed-breed must not know what I have just shown you. It must stay secret. Do you understand? If you go in search of the ferals, you must go alone.*

Duncan was too busy trying to process what he had seen to argue with his mother about Whiski. He had too many questions for her. *How did you find them? Why did you tell them who you were? After everything you taught me!*

Nellie looked hard at her son. *Your second question is an easy one to answer. I was a fool. Trust me, Duncan, for I am your mother, but trust no one else. Blind the mixed-breed. In the long run it is a kindness for her to have never known us for what we truly are. Do not make the same mistakes I did.* Nellie paused. She had very little energy left. *The answer to your first question is much more complicated.* Her eyes met with Duncan's. *The ferals are impossible to find, for they do not wish to be found. I only knew from my relationship with Lenira that they did in fact still exist. I searched for many months looking for clues, but there was nothing. When I had almost given up hope, I had a vision, a vision where I had found them. I searched for the path I had seen. I chose to act on the vision. I cannot say if this was the right choice, but it was the choice I made nonetheless. As you saw from the last vision, the clan has moved, but I do not believe they have gone far. They are the only ones who may know how to help you. In many ways, they know more about our kind than we do. But before you head out on your journey, search your visions, Duncan. If you are meant to find them, then that path will find you. If it does not, do not seek them.*

Duncan embraced his mother. *Thank you,* he whispered.

Nellie hugged him back. *Duncan, please be careful. Every action we take to change our fate carries with it a price. Remember, we must always pay it. I only showed you what I did because I fear the paths facing you that I cannot see. There are many who would wish us harm.*

Duncan buried his face in her fur then turned to go. *Will I see you again?* In his sadness, his flames rose.

Exhausted, she moved to go back inside the house and smiled sadly.

Some things remain hidden, even to the Children of Sagira. Nellie took one last look at her son and was gone.

~

Duncan reached Whiski and stopped. He was brightly lit with flames and consumed by questions. Whiski shook herself to remove the snow that was starting to settle on her coat and shivered. She looked uneasily at Duncan. *You going to put that out?*

Without a word, Duncan knelt to the ground and began to roll in the soft cold mixture of grass, mud, and snow. As he did, the ground turned fully to mud and coated his fur. He pushed himself up from the ground and looked at Whiski.

You look like a farm animal. Her sarcastic expression changed when she saw the weariness in his eyes. *What did she say?*

Duncan began heading back the way they came. *I need to get you home before dawn.*

Whiski moved to block his path. She put her paw on his muddy forehead. *I'm not a human teenager, and I don't have a curfew.*

Duncan remained silent.

Well? What are we going to do? What's the plan?

Duncan shook his head. We *aren't going to do anything.*

Whiski groaned. *Listen here, Dunkelberry, I don't care if you're the reincarnation of Sagira herself. You came into my house, and now you're going to play by my rules.*

Duncan cracked an involuntary smile and looked up at the night sky. *I should have never gotten you involved.*

Whiski smiled back. *True, but you did, and now we're stuck with each other. Start talking, Dunkelberry.*

Duncan looked thoughtfully at Whiski. He thought about his mother's words. Was it a kindness to blind her and disappear forever? Whiski tapped her stub tail impatiently.

Duncan placed his muddy paw on hers. He had trusted her up to this point, and he wasn't going to stop now. *I made you a promise that I would never use any of my powers on you.*

Whiski pulled her paw back. *Hey, don't get any funny ideas, kid! You gave me your word!*

Duncan raised his paws in surrender. *It's just, I just thought maybe you might like to go back home and forget about me.*

Whiski's eyes narrowed. She scooped up a clump of mud and slapped it on top of Duncan's steaming head.

Duncan smiled. *I'll take that as a no.*

Shut up and start talking, Dunkelberry.

~

The two cats made their way toward home while Duncan told her everything he had found out about the ferals, his mother's memories, and finally about her suggestion that he run away. Whiski never interrupted, but instead looked intently forward, nodding occasionally in Duncan's direction, sometimes signaling that they needed to turn at the next hedge. Once he had finished, neither cat spoke for a good 10 minutes. Instead, they walked in silence toward a home that felt as though it was moving farther and farther away.

Whiski finally broke through the silence. *So there's no one who could help? Other than these ancient feral cats, who, by the way, sound really creepy.*

No, Duncan sighed, *just myths and legends.* He kept his gaze at the ground, feeling more hopeless than ever. *I don't know what to do, Whiski. Sit and wait for a vision while I put you all in danger?*

Whiski cleared her throat. *We'll figure something out, kid.*

Duncan looked thoughtfully at his companion. *I actually kind of thought you'd be happy to get rid of me. Thank you...*

Before Whiski could answer, a tortured yowl cut through the night, followed by sounds of human laughter.

Both cats' ears shot back, and they crouched, preparing for an attack.

What was that? mouthed Duncan.

It came from that park over there. Whiski mouthed back.

Duncan began moving in the direction of the noise.

What are you doing? Screaming equals bad! Worse than raccoons! hissed Whiski, running silently after Duncan. *Stay on this side of the road!*

That cat needs help! We can't sit back and do nothing.

Are you crazy? Do you have any idea how dangerous that is? You don't know who is doing that to her or how many there are? You're going to get yourself killed! Actually, no, you're going to get us killed!

Duncan was flicking his tail angrily like a whip. *I am tired of hearing lectures about how dangerous everything is! I'm helping that cat with or without you!*

Whiski growled angrily but continued to move forward with Duncan.

Both cats froze when they saw what was causing the frightening sounds. Two young human males had caught a female cat and were ripping out chunks of her fur and laughing while the cat screamed. Duncan felt his blood begin to heat.

Whiski began to mutter curses under her breath. *Can you blind them?*

Duncan shook his head. *Not before the other one had us. Besides, I have to be up close for that.*

What about persuasion?

I don't think it works on multiple cats or humans at the same time, and now's not the time to find out.

Then what's left!

Duncan let his gold eyes meet Whiski's fierce green ones. *We fight them.*

Whiski frowned. *With what?*

Duncan felt the fire rushing over his shoulders and down his forearms. It burned through the mud almost instantly. It fell like ash around him. *With fire.*

Duncan charged his flaming body at the human holding the cat, leaping and landing squarely on his shoulders. The man screamed as the fire scorched his face and neck. Duncan sank his claws into the man's searing flesh.

Let her go, Duncan hissed.

The man's eyes flickered and he dropped the cat. She had been dangling and twisting in the air. When she hit the ground, she wasted no time fleeing the humans. Whiski came from the shadows and raked her claws across the exposed flesh of the second human. Duncan launched himself off the first man and knocked the other man to the ground. Both men lay writhing around on the asphalt, clutching their burns while trying futilely to knock away their attackers.

Hush.

And the first human was still.

Hush.

And the second human was still.

Duncan covered himself in cool mud again. It acted as a salve against his fiery skin. He found Whiski quickly. She was kicking and cursing at the motionless bodies.

Are you okay?

Whiski nodded. *Filthy excuses for humans. Just leaving some marks for them to remember us by. You?*

Yeah. Duncan exhaled slowly. *I'm okay, but the powers, they're getting stronger. His whiskers flashed in and out of sight.* Whiski used her paws to cover them with mud to mask their erratic visibility. *There,* she grimaced as she looked at him, *that's less noticeable.*

Duncan's eyes caught the movement of the cat they rescued in the bushes. They watched her flinch as she tried to clean her wounds. From the look of her coat, the two humans had been at her awhile. She was a tabby but with the most unusual brown marbled markings. Her coat was long and wild, and her tail hung large and full as a raccoon's. Her feral beauty was marred by the marks left by the men.

Are you okay? asked Duncan cautiously, directing his voice gently into the bushes. He was preparing himself for what he had to do next. She would have seen too much. He had to blind her.

She took a few steps forward and fell to her knees.

We won't hurt you. You're safe now, whispered Whiski.

Son of Sagira. I owe you my life.

Ummm, I'm not... Duncan tried to begin.

You hold the power of flame. You burned my attackers.

I...

Whiski stepped forward to interrupt the girl cat, but the girl was already addressing her.

And you, she bowed to Whiski, *you must be his loyal companion.*

Whiski snorted and pulled at the female cat. *Get up. He's not a Son of Sagira.* She looked at Duncan urgently and blinked suggestively.

Duncan shook his head. They couldn't blind her. He stood quietly, stunned by the turn of events the night had taken. He didn't need to search his visions for the path to the ferals. The path had found him.

The female cat took in their dirty appearances. *I invite you to dine with my family below ground. They will wish to thank you for your kindness.*

187

Before Whiski could answer, Duncan spoke.

Are you of the Feral Clan of Haji? We come in search of the Book of Sagira. Do you know of it?

Whiski's mouth dropped open. She glared and shook her head at Duncan. *Worse than raccoons,* she muttered under her breath.

The girl examined Duncan carefully and then nodded yes. *My father is the keeper of this territory's ancient writings. We guard the Legend of Sagira.* She bowed low again.

*My name is D-*Whiski interrupted, *His name is Dale. I'm Ginger.*

Duncan raised his eyebrows at Whiski but said nothing.

The feral cat bowed again. *I am honored, Dale, Son of Sagira, and Ginger, his trusted companion. You have saved my life, and in return, I shall take you to my home, and I shall lead you to the ancient Writings of Sagira, guarded by my kind for centuries against the purebreds. I am Nafisa, daughter of our colony's leader, Amiri. Follow me.* The feral cat began to lead them through a patch of trees to an open sewer drain. *The humans caught me as I was returning from my hunt. We enter here, but it is still a journey to the clan.*

The girl cat leapt down into the darkness. Before Duncan could follow, Whiski asked him to wait for a second. In a mix between a hiss and a whisper, she spoke anxiously in Duncan's ear. *Are you crazy? We don't know this cat! How are we supposed to trust her?* Duncan lowered his voice. *I have to take the chance.* He raised his already-drying paws to show her the power of the heat flowing through his body. *I can't go back, not like this, not yet.* He looked sadly at Whiski. *I understand if you don't want to come with me.* He placed his paw on hers. *I would never ask you to.* He turned to go, but when he did, Whiski slugged him as hard as she could in the shoulder, gave him a tight smile, and hissed, *Try not to get us killed, Dale.* She jumped down into the shadows after the feral cat. Duncan rubbed his shoulder and smiled. *I'll do my best, Ginger.*

Chapter 24

Franklin's eyes opened slowly. His vision was blurred. Where was he? He tried to move his tongue across his paw, but his throat was so dry that there was no saliva left to wash his face. Franklin lifted his large orange head several inches off the ground. He was in his house, but how did he get here? He was supposed to be on watch, wasn't he? Yes, he remembered heading out into the night and climbing his tree to watch... but then, nothing.

No, not nothing... dark shapes and swirls of color, like a painting, a painting without form.

Franklin looked around him and finally took notice of the warm body lying next to his. Vera... what was she doing here?

Vera? his voice cracked. *Vera?* Franklin nudged his sister. *Vera, wake up.* Her thick brown fur was a mess, tangled and filled with debris. Her eyes were open, yellow and vacant. *Vera!* Franklin's voice rose in panic. He shook his sister. He put his ear next to her chest. She was breathing. Franklin vomited a few pieces of kibble and bile onto the floor. His head was spinning, and his stomach felt like it was on fire. What had happened to them?

Franklin steadied his voice. *Vera! Vera, wake up!* He tried to stand to move closer to her but his knees buckled under his weight. He shook her shoulders more urgently. Still no response.

Franklin looked around the empty room for help. They were alone. Why did he feel like someone else had been in the room with them?

He held his sister's paw gently. His mind raced. Quickly now, Franklin, quickly! What would Varik do? Franklin stopped and whispered to himself, *Perhaps if I use the Guard's Test, she will stir.* He let his claw pierce her pad and felt her blood wet his claw. *Do you bleed the blood that is pure? Please sister, please wake up.*

Vera inhaled sharply and blinked.

Franklin's heart was racing and pounding in relief. He licked her wound and sighed. *I thought I had lost you.*

Vera blinked hard, trying to place where she was. She moved to back away from Franklin but tripped and fell under her weakened limbs. *Who are you? Where am I?*

Sister, it's me, Franklin. Franklin's yellow eyes were watering. They formed dark streaks against the corners of his eyes.

Vera was crouched low, eyes darting around the room. She was breathing heavily and her tail was twitching nervously. She inched backward until she was fully in a corner.

It's okay, you're okay. Franklin stopped moving toward her. Though

191

he tried, he could not contain the tears of panic welling up in his eyes.

I don't know you. Vera shook her head violently. *Where am I?*

Franklin raised his paw and then lowered it when she flinched. *I'm your brother, Franklin. You're in my human's house. You're safe. You are safe, Vera.*

Vera kept looking past Franklin and shaking her head. *I don't know you.*

Vera? Vera, look at me.

Vera jerked back sharply at his words. *You said that before...*

Vera?

Why do you keep calling me that? Who is Vera?

Franklin's shoulders dropped, and rage filled his yellow eyes. He hissed hysterically, *I'll kill them! I'll kill whoever hurt you!*

Vera began to whimper at the sight of Franklin's anger. He stopped immediately when he saw the fear in her face.

No, no, it's okay. I'm sorry, Vera. I should not have yelled. You're okay. I'm sorry. Franklin lowered his head to meet his sister's. *Everything is going to be okay.*

Vera was shaking, but nothing Franklin did seemed to help calm her. He whispered gently to her, pleading with her to come and drink, but she refused to move or speak.

Franklin turned and pulled himself toward his food and water bowls. He collapsed in front of them. He drank deeply, but no amount of water eased the burning in his throat or belly. He needed to be able to walk.

He needed to see Varik. He would be able to help her, wouldn't he? Franklin scolded himself for doubting Varik. Of course he would be able to help Vera. Varik would make sure whoever did this to them paid dearly for it.

Franklin looked over at his sister. When they were kittens, she had been the smallest of the litter, and she was the only chocolate coat among her orange-colored siblings. Franklin used to tease her by calling her, Coco Puff. She would always giggle and tell him that it was better than being a giant Cream Puff like him. Franklin knelt beside her and gently licked her forehead. Vera had always been his favorite sibling, and she had always been the one that protected him, never the other way around.

She stared vacantly past him. He could not reach her, not alone.

Chapter 25

Duncan landed with a thud and splash. He wrinkled his nose. The smell was horrific, like sour milk and week-old meaty mush. He could see almost nothing at first. Though it was dark outside, at least they had the moonlight to guide them. Down here there was only Nafisa's voice. She had climbed back up and pulled closed the sewer cover.

Nafisa spoke in a hushed tone. *Wait a moment and your eyes will adjust.*

In the darkness, Duncan could feel Whiski's glare on him. They were doing their best to breathe through their mouths and not their noses.

Nafisa listened as the two mixed-breeds gagged on the air. *It will not always be so pungent,* she reassured them. *But we must walk a ways to reach my colony. Have your eyes adjusted yet?* Duncan tried to speak, but he could only nod. Nafisa could see and smiled kindly. *Follow me.*

When Nafisa had moved out of earshot, Whiski lowered her voice and hissed. *You owe me big-time, Dunkelberry! This smells worse than any litter box, any garbage*, but before she could finish, Whiski hunched over and vomited. Duncan tried to conceal his smile, *Jeez Ginger, now it's going to smell worse.* Whiski glared at Duncan and pushed him out of her way deeper into the nauseating sewage. *Next time I'll make sure to puke on you,* she grumbled under her breath.

They marched forward through tunnel after tunnel, and just as Nafisa had said, the smell was getting better, or perhaps they had just adjusted to the stench. Duncan was able to start to take in features of his surroundings. When his mother had mentioned that the ferals lived underground, he had imagined something closer to the sewers he had seen on TV, large and filled with sewer mutants and rats. It was nothing like the dark narrow passageways they were traveling. Roaches scuttled across the stone, hissing as they passed over them.

Duncan noticed Nafisa touching markings etched into the walls. He recognized them from his mother's vision.

Nafisa, what are these?

Nafisa paused, trying to decide whether or not to answer. *Signposts to guide our way home. It is difficult to navigate these sewers, so we leave markings that only we can read to lead us home.*

See these markings, she pointed at the stone.

Duncan nodded.

It means we are only about a mile away if we keep heading east.

Whiski paused to examine the marking, and Duncan asked, *What language is this in?*

The ancient language of our ancestors, the original Scribes of Sagira.

None but our kind can read it.

Whiski ran her paw over the marking. *Do you ever worry about the purebreds coming down here?*

Nafisa's voice became heavy. *They prefer to catch us when we come above ground, but they have increased their search for us in recent years. They are why we hunt so far from home, and they are why we move so often. My father has kept us safe here deep in the sewers, but there is more and more pressure for a truce with the purebreds.*

A truce? asked Duncan. *Why would you do that? I thought you hated each other?*

Nafisa grimaced. *You are correct in our mutual hatred, but living in the sewers is difficult, as you could imagine. Many ferals have given up our beliefs and have accepted sanctuary above ground so that they may share territory with the purebreds and the mixed-breeds. Very few clans are left who are devoted to the old ways. Those who are left must live in secrecy. Mine is one of the last,* Nafisa spoke these words proudly, but her voice was tinged with sadness. *Even now, our kind loses their faith.*

Whiski looked down at the sewage moving past them. *What do you mean?* Their breathing had adjusted, though the smell was still sickening.

Nafisa shook her head. *If you give up your history, your culture, all for a bit of fresh air and sunlight against your fur, you dishonor everything we have fought for all these years. I would rather die in the sewers than live in the sun without honor. To forget the past is to lose your faith in the future.*

Sensing the tension in Nafisa's voice, Duncan attempted to quickly change topics. *What of the Book of Sagira? What can you tell me about it?*

Nafisa sighed quietly. *I am sad to say that the purebreds have been successful in erasing much of our history, Son of Sagira. Copies were made of the original Writings of Sagira by feral scribes, but very few copies still remain. Many have been destroyed in pledges of loyalty to the purebreds. They are worth a great deal above ground, but do not worry, we have kept our copy safe for all these years, and we will continue to do so.*

Duncan softened his voice, *Nafisa, what is it about the Book of Sagira that makes you willing to sacrifice so much?*

Duncan could see the outline of a smile on Nafisa's lips. *It is much more than a book. After Sagira was lost to us, our kind did everything we could to preserve what she had given us. Even then, there were those that sought to take the writings from us.* The three cats continued silently through the hot cramped tunnels.

Whiski gave Duncan a jab in the ribs and lowered her voice, *Act a little more like a Son of Sagira!* Duncan frowned at Whiski, though he doubted she could see it. He tried to make his voice sound more commanding. *Tell us more, Nafisa.*

Yes, of course, Son of Sagira, replied Nafisa obediently. *What do you wish to know?*

Duncan cleared his throat, *Umm, more... just, tell us more.*

Whiski gave an annoyed sigh.

Nafisa came to a full stop. *It is said that before Sagira entered the desert, never to be seen again, she sent for Beset, head of the scribes... my ancestor,* the pride in Nafisa's voice carried through the darkness. *Sagira named her protector of the writings, and she told her that the writings must survive, at all costs. Seven copies were made that night, and then each was sent with a group of loyal scribes to ensure its survival after her death.*

Why only seven? asked Duncan.

Nafisa lowered her voice. *It is said that the book contained the magic of Sagira herself. It must not fall into the wrong hands. If they are destroyed, so shall we be destroyed... so it is written, so we are taught. We have devoted our lives to guarding the Book of Sagira so that her magic might survive long enough to fulfill its true purpose.*

What is its true purpose then? asked Whiski skeptically.

Nafisa began walking again. *That I do not know.* She paused. *But Sagira knew its purpose when she gave the book to Beset to protect, and that is good enough for me.*

Duncan frowned. It was sounding less and less likely that this book was going to be of any use to him. Prophecies and magic weren't going to help him control his powers. They weren't going to help him keep his family safe. *She could have made it easier for her children,* Duncan spoke, mostly to himself. *She could have told them what they needed to do, how to survive in a world that didn't want them....*

Nafisa turned her face toward Duncan. He could see only the outline of her body as she spoke. *Sagira saw the entire span of time. Can you imagine the burden she carried, Son of Sagira?* Duncan's fur was smoking from the building heat of his frustration.

She shook her head shamefully. *I am sorry. I have spoken out of turn.*

Whiski interjected quickly. *Have you read the Book of Sagira?*

Of course not, replied Nafisa.

Duncan and Whiski exchanged confused glances.

Nafisa started again. *Perhaps I can explain. It is not for my eyes. It is my job to keep it safe. The Book is for the Children of Sagira. We will preserve it for as long as the purebreds seek to destroy it.*

Well that stinks, muttered Whiski.

Duncan nudged Whiski. She shrugged back and whispered, *Well, it does.*

Duncan tried to hide his disappointment but failed. Nafisa eyed him curiously. Whiski quickly interrupted the silence. *How close are we to your home?*

Close. Nafisia's nose was bright pink as she turned away from Duncan. *We should reach them a few hours before dawn. My father will want to honor you both over a meal. You may stay with us as long as you wish while you study the Book of Sagira.*

Though neither cat could imagine spending any more time than necessary down in the sewers, Duncan and Whiski nodded in what they hoped looked like an appreciative gesture.

Hey, Nafisa? Asked Whiski.

Yes, Ginger, loyal companion of Dale?

Whiski grumbled under her breath, *Just Ginger is fine.*

Nafisa smiled. *Yes, Ginger?*

Out of curiosity, have you, or anyone in your colony, ever met a Child of Sagira before?

No, why do you ask?

Duncan's golden eyes flickered in the dark. Had they not known what his mother was?

Whiski continued. *Well then, how are you sure they will welcome us with open arms?*

They will honor you, as I honor you both. You need not worry. Nafisa picked up her pace.

Whiski shot Duncan a look of concern. Duncan ignored her and moved faster to match Nafisa's stride. They could not afford to turn back now.

~

Nafisa stopped and placed her paw on the concrete, or what Duncan thought was concrete. She tapped her claws in a musical pattern. It sounded like a mouse playing a snare drum. When she had finished, the concrete slid open.

What on Earth? muttered Whiski.

It's not really concrete, whispered Nafisa over her shoulder. *It's dark plastic that we salvaged out of the trash. We roughed it up until it looked right. There's a guard on the other side who listens for the password. Pretty good, huh?* Nafisa grinned. She had surprisingly bright eyes and white little teeth for someone who lived her life wading through sewage.

Duncan nodded. He and Whiski stood on the other side of the hole staring at Nafisa, who had already passed through.

It's safe, I assure you. Come quickly.

Whiski gestured at Duncan, *You first.*

Duncan inhaled deeply. This was a small hole, and he was no longer a kitten.

Whiski smiled at Duncan who was trying to figure out the right angle to stuff his body through. *Do I need to grease you up, kid?*

Duncan waved his butt in her face and then went for it. It was tight around the gut, but he made it.

Nafisa nodded at the hole. *There are very few purebreds who can fit through that.*

Duncan's eyes narrowed as he thought of Franklin.

Whiski wiggled through with little trouble.

Nafisa nodded to the guard, and he replaced the plastic.

The guard looked suspiciously at Duncan and Whiski but said nothing.

Whiski whispered in Duncan's ear. *This place is creepy. I say you read that book, and we get the out of here as fast as we can.*

Duncan nodded. He had to admit, this place was like something out of an Indiana Jones movie. At least he hadn't seen any snakes yet.

They continued on through a short dark tunnel. The sound of running water, if you could call it water, echoed against the low concrete ceilings.

Almost. Nafisa turned and the three of them emerged into a large cavern. Duncan blinked hard. It appeared the ferals were quite clever at reusing items discarded by humans. There were battery-powered lanterns and flashlights scattered throughout the room to create a soft yellow light that filled the space. Duncan could see old couch pillows and torn mattress pads strewn over the floor.

Whiski moved closer to Duncan. At first, he wasn't sure if it was a sign of fear or an attempt at protection, but then he realized what held her stare. At least 20 pairs of eyes were staring at them from the shadows. The surroundings were so dark that only a thin ring of color outlined the black orbs that made up their eyes. There were cats of all ages, but even the kittens managed to look old. Their stomachs were swollen from hunger, and many of the cats looked like they were suffering from parasites. Their faces were thin and their coats were ragged.

Nafisa stepped in front of them and spoke clearly and with force. *I have returned with two guests. They saved my life.* Nafisa paused, letting her colony take in her damaged coat.

A large figure stepped forward from the shadows. He was huge but lean, a dark grey tabby with disturbingly large and fearsome looking paws. Duncan swallowed hard and wondered briefly how he got through the hole. His thoughts were halted by the power in the grey tabby's voice.

My child, we do not entertain guests. Even ones to whom we owe our lives.

Nafisa bowed deeply. *Father, he is a Son of Sagira.* Duncan could hear the gasps from the cats in the room. *He was born from the fire. He fought my attackers with flame. I witnessed it with my own eyes.* Nafisa gestured at Whiski. *She is his companion. She fought bravely alongside him.*

The grey tabby's eyes widened. They were a cloudy green, speckled with flecks of brown, but they brightened when they looked at Duncan.

Whiski took another step toward Duncan.

Forgive me, he bowed. *I am Amiri, Father of Nafisa, and leader of our colony, Haji.*

Nafisa dipped her head suggestively at Duncan and Whiski.

They both bowed nervously. Duncan looked at Whiski. The look that she gave him made it clear that he was going to have to do the talking.

I am honored to meet you, Amiri, Father of Nafisa, leader of the colony, Haji. I am Dale, Son of Sagira, and this is my companion, Ginger.

Amiri bowed again. *I apologize, Son of Sagira, I did not mean you any offense. We lead solitary lives here in the sewers. We are not used to company.*

Amiri looked up at Whiski and smiled at her aggressive stance. *I apologize to you as well, Ginger, loyal companion of Dale.*

Whiski huffed in annoyance but nodded grudgingly. She relaxed her shoulders, but only slightly.

Duncan raised himself up so that he sat taller. He cleared his throat. *We seek the Book of Sagira. Nafisa tells me that you guard a copy.*

Amiri's face became serious. He looked questioningly at his daughter. *Yes, this is true, but you must be hungry. We were just about to sit down to eat. Come, join us... then, once you have rested, we shall talk of Sagira.*

Duncan began to protest and then thought better of it.

203

Nafisa approached her father, and he gently touched where she had had her fur ripped from her skin.

We are grateful. Amiri looked up from his daughter's damaged coat. *We are grateful to you both.*

Duncan looked intensely at Amiri, but he did not see any deceit in his eyes, only sadness.

Duncan and Whiski followed Amiri and Nafisa through a second tunnel connecting to another, large room.

There were dead rats and various garbage items piled in the center of the room. Cats began to file in quickly. Whiski stayed close to Duncan's side. She was trying to keep her face expressionless, but he could tell she was freaked out. The truth was, Duncan was beginning to feel that way himself. Perhaps the lack of sleep and food was beginning to wear his courage thin. He looked at Whiski. They couldn't speak freely to one another; there were too many cats here for that. Instead, they stood in silence as Nafisa explained their food rituals.

Soon my father will approach the group, ask for silence, and then he and the council will begin to pass out the rations.

Council? asked Duncan

Yes, my father is the leader of the colony, but the other senior members of the clan hold positions of power as well. Together, they make up the council. They are called the Khalfani.

Why is everyone so quiet? he whispered.

Nafisa lowered her voice. *They have never seen a Son of Sagira before. You are... well... you are a legend brought to life. It is a lot to take in all at once.*

Yes, replied Duncan dryly, *Yes, it is.*

Whiski added thoughtfully. *It must be strange to devote your whole life to protecting something... all for these mythical cats you've never even met.*

Nafisa narrowed her eyes and stiffened her body. The words came out of her throat in almost a hiss. *Not if you choose to live with honor.*

Duncan thought he saw her looking at a ginger shorthair across the room while she spoke, but he couldn't be sure.

Amiri walked to the center of the room. The cats had formed a circle around him.

Colony, welcome. His voice boomed and echoed across the walls. *We are blessed to have received one of our daughters home safely from the hunt. We are blessed to have with us today a child born of the fire, a Son of Sagira....*

He is here to save us! cried an elderly calico cat. *He will save us from the purebreds!*

And the hunger in our bellies! cried another.

Duncan's ears went back. Save them? He began to shake his head, but Whiski nudged him.

Silence! scolded Amiri. *We do not welcome our guests by making demands!*

Duncan looked over at the tomcat Nafisa had been directing her anger toward. The ginger cat kept his eyes focused on Duncan. His nose was extremely pale, and his right ear torn almost half way off. He smiled at Duncan and then spoke.

Perhaps a demonstration? he spoke clearly and loudly. *It has been my life's dream to meet one of your kind, to see the power you have been blessed with.*

Dukatt! barked Amiri.

Nafisa yelled out. *We are here to serve! He is not here to do our bidding!*

Why should you be angry, Nafisa? replied the ginger cat slyly. *Does our guest object?*

I object to your rudeness! growled Amiri.

Duncan gulped. He was trying not to start shaking. Whiski was digging her claws into the ground to keep her emotions in check.

Please! Please show us! a small black kitten near Duncan mewed softly up at him.

Duncan looked at Whiski, then at Nafisa, and finally at Amiri. Amiri shook his head. Duncan exhaled in relief.

He looked around at the crowd and suddenly became extremely self-conscious. He hoped that all his body parts were still visible. The mud was starting to dry and crack. He was beginning to feel the heat building again. The faces in the crowd, they were difficult to read. Some were elated; others looked as though they were going to burst into tears at any moment; and some simply looked angry. Duncan inhaled deeply to try to slow his rapidly beating heart. Yes, it was better when their faces were hidden in shadow.

Khalfani, members of the council! boomed Amiri. *Please join me in distributing the rations.* Amiri lifted a large rat and carried it over to Duncan and Whiski and dropped it at their feet. Quickly the rest of the council followed his lead distributing rats and garbage. Duncan looked down at the rat. He had never seen anything so upsetting in his life. Its worm-like tail flopped across his paw. He was sure he was going to throw up.

Whiski glared at him. *Don't you dare! There's no meaty mush here,* she hissed into Duncan's ear. With great skill, she began to filet the rat. She whispered again, this time more kindly. *Really, kid, they're not that bad. Rat actually tastes a lot like chicken.*

Duncan scowled. *Chickens come in "crispy" or "original recipe," and they don't have tails.*

Whiski chuckled. Within minutes, she had two piles of rat meat stacked in front of them. Nafisa smiled expectantly over at Duncan. He plastered a fake grin on his face and shoved a large piece of rat into his mouth and chewed.

He gulped. Oh, dear.

Whiski! He hissed urgently.

Whiski glared at him.

I mean, Ginger!

What? She hissed back.

This meat is r-a-w.

Whiski stared at him.

I mean, it's not cooked!

She started snickering, trying to suppress her laughter.

Duncan glared at her, confused.

Kid, it's supposed to be raw. Eat it.

Duncan looked over at Nafisa and then sadly back down at the rat. He apprehensively picked up another bite.

Whiski lifted her rat morsel. *To Sagira.*

Duncan couldn't help but smile. He raised his rat meat. *To Sagira.*

Chapter 26

The meal passed quickly, and Duncan was relieved to have kept his portion down. Whiski, oddly enough, seemed to be enjoying herself.

As she cleaned her claws, she purred. *Ah, nothing like fresh, well, mostly fresh, meat. You know we're supposed to eat this stuff raw, right? Humans are the ones who started cooking our food.*

Duncan grimaced and rubbed his belly. *Well, remind me to thank them when we get home then.*

Whiski poked at Duncan's belly. *Who's the frumpy middle-aged house cat now?*

Amiri approached them and bowed. *Was your meal to your liking?*

Duncan stiffened and forced an awkward grin. Whiski bowed back. *It was delicious.*

Amiri smiled. *May I offer you seconds?*

Duncan patted his belly, *Oh no, no... we're full,* he answered quickly. Whiski frowned but nodded.

Then please, let me show you our colony. He gestured with his striped plume of a tail for them to follow.

Duncan looked at Whiski and she shrugged. They walked slowly behind Amiri as he spoke to them over his shoulder.

The other ferals backed up and bowed, making a path for them to walk.

Whiski began to protest when Amiri stopped her. *It is our place to honor the Children of Sagira. You bring them great joy.*

Whiski narrowed her eyes in disapproval but said nothing.

Duncan scanned the faces for the tomcat he had seen in his mother's vision, but he wasn't among the crowd that bowed before them.

Amiri led them through a small tunnel into a separate room. He pointed to the walls. Where there had been crumbling bricks, small caves had been fashioned into the walls. There had to be at least ten to fifteen in this room. A small camping lantern had been placed in the center of the room.

This is where we rest, spoke Amiri quietly. *Of course, you have already seen our common area as well as the prey room.*

Duncan nodded and looked around him in awe.

How long have you been living underground? He asked.

Amiri sighed heavily. *That is a difficult question. Time feels as though it passes differently down here. We have lived beneath the rest of the world for the entirety of my life.* He continued. *But this was not always so. After the Dark Times, we lived alone in the wild, guarding our territory with tooth and claw. But then, as the humans pressed farther and farther out, we had fewer and fewer places to hide. The purebreds and the humans both pursued us. The humans believed us to be carriers of disease, and so they hunted us. We began our slow retreat into the depths of the earth. It has been this way for several generations, including mine, and I fear for my daughter's as well. But make no mistake, we are nomads in this world. We seek shelter only for a short time, and we flee danger when at first its grim shadow appears.*

There are more important things than our lives that must be kept safe.

Amiri led them through yet another series of tunnels. *We are descendants of the Scribes of Sagira, and we carry on our backs the secrets of the past, long destroyed in the world above us.*

Amiri? asked Duncan thoughtfully.

Yes, Son of Sagira?

Can you tell me what is within the Book of Sagira?

Amiri was silent at first, and when he spoke, his voice sounded tired. *That is a very great question.*

Whiski spoke cautiously but firmly. *It was evidently too great a question for your daughter to tell us on our trip here. Have you not read the book either?*

Amiri chuckled. *Ginger, you are a spirited one. I can see why the Son of Sagira chooses your company. You are not afraid to speak your mind.*

Duncan smiled apologetically at Amiri and then glared at Whiski. *No, she is most definitely not.* Whiski gave Duncan an annoyed sigh and

211

then turned back to Amiri. *I meant no disrespect, of course, but for devoting your whole lives to protecting this thing, it seems like you don't know very much about it, just stories that you've been passing down for ages.*

Amiri smiled. Duncan was relieved he was amused by Whiski. Amiri directed his response to the both of them. *The answer is that no, I have not read the Writings of Sagira, but my father did. He made the last copy when the previous book was fading.* He lowered his voice. *But Son of Sagira, I can tell you this. The Book of Sagira is said to contain the great prophecies of Sagira. It tells of her five powers and of the fate of her children. In it, she foretells their fall into darkness, but she also speaks of their rebirth. That is why the purebreds will do anything to obtain the last remaining copies of the book. They fear the return of the Children of Sagira. They fear the magic in her words.*

Both Whiski and Duncan exchanged glances. Whiski spoke softly, *I'm not sure we're following exactly.*

Amiri nodded. *During their service, the feral scribes recorded words spoken by Sagira. As more and more of the things that Sagira spoke of came to pass, the scribes began to worship her words as prophecy. Sagira's words are difficult to interpret.* Amiri looked back at Duncan. *Perhaps they have been waiting for you all this time.*

Whiski frowned. *What language are these writings in?*

They are written in our old hand... the language you have seen marking your way to this colony.

Duncan's eyes narrowed in concern. He hadn't thought of the fact that the writings may not be in a language he could read. Whiski was

212

obviously thinking the same thing because she sighed deeply.

Have I said something to displease you, little Ginger?

Whiski's ears flicked forward. *No, well... we... he*, she pointed at Duncan, *was hoping to read it.*

Amiri looked at Duncan curiously.

Would you translate it for him? asked Whiski.

Amiri raised his ears in surprise. *Of course, if he asked it of me.*

Whiski nodded, *When can we do that?*

This time Duncan interrupted. *What do you know of the five powers of Sagira.*

Amiri chuckled again at the two companions. *What do you wish to know?*

Have you ever heard of... I don't know, a Child of Sagira having a couple different powers?

Amiri's tail flicked dismissively. *No, of course not. Legend dictates that each child after Sagira only inherits one of her powers, and it has been that way ever since. Why do you ask?*

Duncan shrugged his shoulders. *Just curious. Besides, how do you really know that...*

Whiski interrupted him. *This place is like a maze.*

Amiri paused for a brief second and then smiled. *It is not so difficult to navigate once you are accustomed to living below ground. The pipes and tunnels of the sewers are your human streets.*

Duncan started to speak, but Whiski cut him off. *We have actually lived in many places, but none quite like this.* She gave Duncan a knowing look, and Duncan nodded. She was probably right to be cautious, but he couldn't help but trust Amiri. There was something about the way Amiri looked at them that made Duncan believe he meant no harm.

Amiri continued down a long tunnel to another new room. Unlike the previous rooms, this one was guarded by two ferals sitting at the entrance. Amiri turned and bowed again. *You have already given me much by giving me my daughter back, but I wish to ask one more thing of you. Would you please be our honored guest at our council meeting? Our clan is in great need of your wisdom.*

Whiski snorted at the reference to Duncan's wisdom, but Duncan nodded as formally as he could. The guards parted, and Duncan and Whiski followed Amiri into the Council of Khalfani.

~

Duncan thought that this room was the most unsettling one he had been in so far. It was dimly lit, and a small group of five elder ferals was seated in a circle around a large drawing of what Duncan imagined to be Sagira and her five children.

Amiri bowed, and Duncan and Whiski followed his lead. There was silence when the council noticed Amiri had not come alone. Duncan raised his head and recognized a familiar pair of green eyes staring back at him. It was the tomcat from his mother's vision. Duncan quickly looked down at the ground, but he could feel the tomcat staring intensely at him.

Amiri entered into the empty spot in the sixth seat and spoke to the group. *I have with me a great guest to the council: Dale, Son of Sagira, child born of fire, and Ginger, his faithful companion. For the duration of their stay here, I propose that they are given full speaking rights in the council. Let us vote. Raise your tail if you are in favor of allowing full rights to be given to our two honored guests.*

Duncan watched as the elders voted. Four tails in favor of yes. Only Dukatt, the ginger cat toward whom Nafisa had directed so much hatred during dinner, and the green-eyed tomcat from his mother's vision, kept their tails down.

Then it is settled. Amiri's voice echoed in the small cavern. *Have a seat of your choosing.*

Duncan sat down exactly where he stood. He had no interest in moving away from Amiri. Whiski sat carefully down beside him. She scanned the room for the guards. They had retaken their place blocking the exit.

~

Dukatt, Amiri spoke dryly, *you wished to bring something forward to the council for a vote today?*

Dukatt looked at Duncan and smiled. *Why yes, thank you, Amiri.*

Dukatt stepped into the center of the circle. *Too long have we spent our lives underground. Though you may choose not to see it,* he looked at Amiri, *there is decay all around us. Kittens are starving. Those who have survived to adulthood are gravely ill. Our hunters bring back less and less food each time, and some do not return at all. I ask the council to answer me why we continue to suffer here below ground, all in the name of Sagira?* Dukatt looked directly at Duncan. *Perhaps the Son of Sagira can answer me?*

Dukatt, spoke another member of the council, *you know why we continue to serve in the ways of old. Is the Son of Sagira standing before you not proof enough of this?*

The ways of old! The ways of old involved living in Egyptian palaces, or even in the Dark Times we were able to breathe fresh air! My friend, there is no farther to fall! We have lost. Let us bring tribute to the purebreds. Let us escape the curse of our past while we still can!

I have heard enough! roared Amiri. *How many more times must you tempt the council to act in heresy?*

Until the council sees reason, returned Dukatt defiantly.

One of the other members of the council turned to Duncan. *What would you have us do, Son of Sagira?* The cat from his mother's vision said nothing.

Suddenly, all eyes were on Duncan. *I...I,* Duncan stopped. *I would not have my words guide the fate of your lives.*

You see! yelled Dukatt. *No words of comfort, not even from the mouth of the Son of Sagira!*

Duncan spoke, and he was surprised by the power in his voice. *I came here seeking the Book of Sagira. Your future is your own to make, as is mine. I am no god, and I have my own battles to fight. Please leave me out of yours.*

The ferals were quiet. Amiri finally spoke. *Wise words, indeed, from the Son of Sagira. We are behaving like petty kittens without honor.* He looked pointedly at Dukatt.

Amiri exhaled heavily. *Let us vote then. Tails up if you wish to leave the sewers and abandon our service to Sagira.*

Duncan and Whiski stayed close to each other.

Only one cat raised his ginger tail. Dukatt whispered. *So be it.*

Amiri lowered his voice. *Meeting dismissed.*

Amiri signaled for Duncan and Whiski to wait as the rest of the council cleared out. The last to leave, the tomcat from his mother's vision paused as he passed by Duncan. For a moment, Duncan had nearly called out to him, but as their eyes met and he saw the alarm in the tomcat's green eyes, he thought better of it.

Once the council had left, Amiri bowed once again to Duncan. *I apologize for Dukatt's anger. He was once quite an honorable cat, but now he suffers cruelly from the loss of his wife. But you are right, you came here for your own purpose, and I shall not impose the burdens of my clan upon you. I shall aid you the best I can in translating the Book of Sagira. Meet me in our common space in an hour, and I shall help you find your answers.*

Chapter 27

It was almost dawn. Franklin was taking a chance. He knew that. But Vera was not improving. He had to see Varik

After much coaxing, Franklin had managed to convince Vera to eat and drink a little something. He led her back to a rarely used corner of his human's house. He had dragged one of his portable beds and a towel from the guest bathroom to keep her warm. She quickly passed back into unconsciousness. It had taken Franklin the better part of an hour and a half to get the use of his limbs back. And even still, he was painfully sore and stiff. With a great deal of effort, he was able to maintain a sort of hobbling motion capable of taking him as far as he needed to go.

He was forced to stop and rest several times, but Franklin made himself keep moving clumsily down the familiar path to Varik's house. Straining, he moved to push the window open. Surely Varik would understand. His sister needed him. She had always served the guard faithfully. Franklin pushed through the window frame and landed with a crash into the house. It was dark, but he could make out some shapes.

Franklin, a voice barely above a whisper broke though the silence.

Varik? I can't see you. Varik, where are you?

Why are you here, Franklin? You have entered my home uninvited. Surely, you know better than that.

Sir! My sister! We've been attacked! Franklin was speaking frantically now into the darkness. Why wouldn't Varik show himself?

Franklin was stumbling over his words in panic. *We were out patrolling, or, I guess I was out patrolling, and then... well, and then we both woke up back in my human's house. My sister and I were, I mean, I am weak, Varik, I know that, but my sister, she needs your help! She cannot remember who she is! Someone has done this to her!*

Quiet, you foolish, fluffy oaf! Varik leapt out from the shadows, his whip-like tail, his green eyes, his ruddy coat, all shone magnificently in the soft early-morning light.

Explain to me what has happened, and slowly. He hissed out the words. *You are a member of my guard. Act like one!*

Yes, Varik, Franklin bowed his head and took a deep breath. He told Varik the rest of the story, at least the parts he could remember.

Let me see if I understand you correctly. You were attacked in the night, but you have no memory of who did this to you?

And Vera, sir.

219

Yes, and Vera has been driven mad.

Varik stared past Franklin. He turned and started walking back into the shadows. Still deep in thought, he whispered. *Bring her to me.*

Franklin fell to the floor in gratitude. *Thank you, Varik.* He knew he dared not say any more. He hurried his fat orange body toward home with the goal of returning with Vera before full sunrise.

~

Varik paced in his dark basement. It can't be, can it?

He moved fluidly across the room. A child of Sagira, alive, after all these years? And not only alive, but here, in my territory? Impossible. Varik shook his head. His superiors would think he was joking when he reported this. It had been over 15 years since the last Child of Sagira had been sighted anywhere, outside of even the memories of his elders. Varik could feel his normally controlled mind burning with curiosity. He must not be hasty. He had been hasty once before in his youth, and his reward had been the band of fools now under his command. No, first he must see Vera. He must have proof, and then, only then, could he act without the risk of angering his superiors.

He rubbed his forehead with a ruddy paw. A child of sight... the most dangerous of them all, save Sagira herself. To have any hope of victory, he would have to move quickly, using the ways of old. He sat down on the cool marble floor to think. He had been waiting for years for an opportunity like this. Ever since he was a young tom, he had dreamt of rising in the ranks of the purebred guard. He had devoted his life to being a loyal soldier. Perhaps, after all this time, fate had finally seen fit to reward him.

He scoured his mind for any other explanation, but he could find none. The pathetic lump of a Persian and his sister showed signs of being touched by the power of sight. Varik looked out into the early morning and let his pupils contract from the brightness of the snow still left on the ground. Could anything else inflict that kind of damage on a cat? Varik mused to himself. Franklin, well, Franklin could be taken down by an irate squirrel, but Vera, no... Varik shook his head. Vera was a strong fighter. Whoever did this to them had to have been more than just a cat.

But whoever stopped it... Varik ran his claw through the middle of a spider moving silently across the floor... *would be a hero*, he whispered. Smiling, he watched its legs twitch as it died.

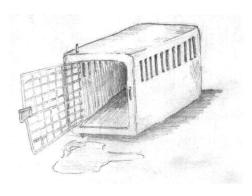

Chapter 28

Duncan and Whiski spoke in hurried whispers in the feral common room. They stopped short when the ginger cat, Dukatt, skulked forward.

Dale, is it?

Duncan nodded and cleared his throat. *Yes, that's me, and this is Ginger.*

The expression on the ginger cat's face was arrogant. *I am Dukatt. I am honored to meet you.*

Yeah, uh, you too.

Dukatt smiled. He was missing one of his fangs.

Please do not take what I said in the council personally. I care only for the health and well-being of my colony. Unfortunately, Amiri and I differ in our opinions, but please, I hope that shall not color your opinion of me. In fact, I have already spoken to Amiri and apologized for my outburst at the council. I spoke passionately yet inappropriately. To begin to make amends for my behavior, Amiri has asked me to escort you to your quarters so that you may rest. You must both be very weary from your journey.

Whiski's voice was wary. *What do you mean by quarters? Amiri said we were supposed to meet here.*

Your servant is outspoken, replied Dukatt coldly.

Duncan could tell that Whiski wanted desperately to knock Dukatt flat on his back.

She's not my servant.

Sorry?

She's--Not—My--Servant.

Goodness, my apologies, Dukatt smiled contemptuously at Whiski. *I just assumed a Son of Sagira would have someone to wait on him.*

Whiski was too furious to speak.

To your quarters then?

Duncan looked for Amiri or Nafisa in the crowd, but they were nowhere to be found.

Yeah, fine. To our quarters.

Excellent. Dukatt signaled to two guards.

Is that really necessary? Whiski spoke in a voice close to a hiss.

Anything for your protection, crooned Dukatt.

The five of them walked down a dark tunnel leading to an unfamiliar section of the colony's lair. They continued for what felt like quite a ways. They emerged into a small area with several cages. They looked like they had been dragged out of the garbage down into the sewers, some house cat's discarded pet taxi.

This is wrong, thought Duncan. But before either cat could act, the guards had struck them hard in the back of their heads. Disoriented, they were shoved into a crate, and the door was slammed shut.

Dukatt spat in his face. *You are no Son of Sagira, and I owe you nothing.*

~

Wake up! Wake up, Duncan! Whiski whispered in a panic while she shook Duncan's shoulders.

Duncan's eyes opened slowly. *What... what happened?*

Whiski held Duncan's face in her paws and began examining him. *Are you hurt?*

Ouch! Duncan winced as Whiski's paw ran over the lump forming on the back of his head.

Sorry! I think you're going to be okay though. They hit us pretty hard. I was worried about you when you didn't wake up right away.

The guard standing closest to them sneered at Duncan and Whiski. *Did Baby Boy Sagira hurt his head?*

Whiski growled and threw herself against the cage door, wrapped her claws around the bars, and yelled back. *Come over here and say that!*

The large tomcat approached. His fur was scraggly, and he was black and tan in a marbled pattern that moved across his face like a mask. His

224

eyes were sunken, and his teeth shown yellow when he leered at them. *Settle down! Or do you need me to teach you a lesson, little girl?*

I'd like to see you try! hissed Whiski.

Jabari, don't forget father's orders. A thin female ginger cat put her paw on her brother's shoulder. *Leave them be. They will not be our concern much longer. Father will return soon, and we must be ready, and they,* she gestured to Duncan and Whiski with her tail, *must be in one piece.*

Jabari gave Whiski one last look of disgust before he turned to join his sister.

Whiski, whispered Duncan, *what's going on?* He was still having trouble focusing his eyes.

She shook her head. *I don't know, but it doesn't look good.*

Duncan raised himself to look around the abandoned pet-taxi-turned-prison. It was filthy and covered in a thick layer of dirt and grime that rubbed off on their fur when they touched it.

Whiski whispered in his ear, *Can you use your gift on them?*

If they both look at me, yeah, I think I can. But I don't know how we're going to get out of here once I do. This place is a maze, not to mention this cage. I... but before he could finish, Dukatt entered the room.

Ah, my little imposters are awake, I see. Children, watch the door. We may have visitors soon. Jabari and his sister nodded and moved to the opening of the tunnel.

Duncan growled. *Why are you doing this?*

Dukatt laughed dryly. *Why am I doing this? An excellent question.*

He leapt forward and hit the cage hard with his paw, his eyes wild with suppressed anger. Dukatt composed himself and turned to keep his eyes focused on the tunnel. *I am doing this so that we may live free above ground as we were meant to... free of ancient lies that bring only suffering and death. I am doing this because the council refuses to see reason. But mostly, I am doing this because, thanks to you, I finally have a chance to get my family out of this horrid place once and for all!*

What do you mean? hissed Whiski. *What do you want with us?*

I simply want to make a trade.

Duncan rammed his body against the door, and the cage lurched forward.

Now, now, don't tire yourself out. Amiri will want to know that you're alive and well if he's going to hand over the Book of Sagira to save you. He believes you're the real thing, you know.

Duncan stopped. He was breathing heavily trying to keep himself from catching fire.

Whiski's eyes widened. *I can't believe it.* She shook her head. *You're going to give the book to the purebreds in exchange for their protection above ground. That's the tribute you were talking about during the meeting!*

Dukatt smiled sarcastically. *I couldn't have done it without you*

Duncan growled. *How could you do this to your colony?*

Dukatt's hackles rose in indignation. *Me? My people have done this to themselves! They believe with all their loyal, stupid little hearts that they serve the Children of Sagira by hiding down here in this sewage pit.*

And do you want to know the funny part? Even as they watch their children grow sick and die from living in these vile conditions, they still manage to believe in the power of the ancient myths. They have sacrificed the lives of generations upon generations of cats, all to protect a moldy old book. And they do all of this in the name of Sagira. Dukatt laughed humorlessly. *I have done nothing but serve my entire life, and I finally figured it out. It's all a lie, but my children... no, my children will not be slaves to a myth.*

Duncan spoke each word sharply. *We do exist. My real name is Duncan, and I am a Son of Sagira. I am asking you to let us go.*

Dukatt snorted in disbelief. *Well, at first I thought you two were just very clever cats set out to trick my colony into giving you their sacred book so you could sell it on the market. But now, now I see that you really are as crazy as the rest of these fools. You actually think you're a Son of Sagira.* He laughed harder.

Duncan, Duncan, stay calm, Whiski whispered urgently in his ear. She could feel the heat radiating from his body. If he burst into flames while they were both trapped in the carrier, the fire would consume them both.

Duncan lowered his voice, *Say that to my face, Dukatt. Tell me I'm not a Son of Sagira. I want to see the doubt flash in your eyes when you realize your mistake.*

Dukatt turned just enough to spit at Duncan's feet. *Maybe some other time. Right now, you wait. Your "followers" will be arriving soon.*

~

About an hour passed while Duncan and Whiski waited in the cramped cage. Duncan was starting to feel seriously ill. He hadn't slept in over

12 hours, unless you count the time he spent knocked unconscious, and the effort of trying to suppress the fire was taking its toll on him. His mud was almost completely cracked off.

Hold on, Whiski panted in the growing heat. *Just hold on, kid.*

Duncan nodded, too tired to speak.

They had watched messages being carried back and forth between their cave's tunnel and the feral colony for what seemed like an eternity when Amiri emerged holding a small black leather book, bound by a strap that he held in his teeth. Duncan sat up straighter. The Book of Sagira!

Whiski watched Duncan nervously. She wasn't sure how much longer they could stay in this cage before he lost control and burst into flames.

Amiri's eyes left Dukatt's only for a brief moment to account for Duncan and Whiski.

He dusted the ground clean with his large tail and then gently set the book down on the ground. He kept his paw on the book to indicate he still had possession.

Ah, Amiri! Good, you finally came.

You shame us all, Dukatt, Amiri whispered sadly.

Jabari growled, but his sister held him back.

That is where you are wrong, Amiri, hissed back Dukatt. *I take care of my family.*

We are your family.

Family, sneered Dukatt, *My family stands behind me. Where were you when my wife lay dying down in this filth? Daylight will never touch her fur. What kind of family allows that?*

Dukatt, this is not the answer.

Oh, no? Dukatt's voice was becoming strained. *You know, my wife believed in your stories, Amiri, but I do not. This cannot continue. My children will be free of this. Hand over the book!*

Amiri eyed Duncan. *Release them.*

Dukatt shook his head. *Give my daughter the book. Let her and her brother leave here, and do not pursue them. Once they are out of your reach, I will release your precious savior.*

Father? cried Jabari in surprise.

Amiri looked with pity at Jabari. *Child, did you not see that all three of you would never be allowed to leave here alive?*

Jabari ignored Amiri and instead pleaded with Dukatt, *Father, there must be another way!*

Dukatt's voice was quiet but stern. *None that would see both you and your sister alive and safe above ground. I have given your sister instructions for where to take the book. Aissa, do you remember everything I have told you?*

Aissa bowed her head. *Yes, father.*

Jabari looked in shock at his sister.

The book! commanded Dukatt.

Amiri's face was so pained that Duncan had to turn away. This was wrong, this was all wrong!

Amiri pushed the book forward and Dukatt carried it in his teeth to his daughter. He licked both children once on the head. *Now go!*

Duncan strained to make eye contact with the children, but their eyes were fixed on their father's.

Jabari shook his head, but Dukatt's stony face made him turn to follow his sister. She quickly moved another hidden door, and both cats disappeared into a tunnel leading out of the feral colony, carrying the book upon which Duncan had placed all of his hopes for a normal life.

Once they disappeared from view, Dukatt sneered. *See Amiri, my children will live free of your lies.* He turned. Amiri was already starting to circle Dukatt.

I shall last long enough, Amiri. I will not let you kill me until they have had enough time to escape.

We shall see, Dukatt. Amiri lunged forward and raked a set of sharp claws across Dukatt's flank. Dukatt's ears fell back and he unsheathed his own claws for the fight he was sure to lose.

My daughter pursues your children as we speak, Amiri hissed.

You lie! growled Dukatt.

Never, replied Amiri, *never about this.* He lunged and grabbed ahold of Dukatt's neck as the two wrestled to gain advantage over the other.

Duncan started hyperventilating. *It's too much, Whiski! I can't stop it.*

You have to! Whiski yelled over the roar of Amiri and Dukatt battling each other. But before she could finish, Duncan's tail was ablaze, and it was spreading quickly forward. Whiski was banging on the cage latch.

Amiri! Duncan cried.

Both fighting tomcats looked up, but only Dukatt stopped fighting to stare in wonder at Duncan.

You're real, he whispered in shock. He felt Amiri's limbs close around his neck. *Forgive me, Son of Sagira.*

And with one jerk, Dukatt's neck was broken, and Amiri was racing to open the carrier.

Whiski tumbled out and jumped into the sewer water to put out her singed fur, while Duncan stood, consumed by his own fire. His golden eyes were filled with anger and pity as he stared down at the body of the Dukatt.

~

We must hurry, urged Amiri. *There is not much time. Once they have reached the surface, we will have lost them.*

What about Nafisa? asked Whiski.

She is pursuing them through another set of tunnels, but I fear it may be too late.

He took off running through the hidden tunnel, and Whiski and Duncan were hard pressed to keep up with his pace through its twists and turns in the dark.

There is still a chance, Duncan kept repeating to himself, but deep down he couldn't help feeling that everything was lost.

No! cried Amiri, as they reached the end of the tunnel and came skidding to a halt. The brightness of early morning light was blinding.

231

All three cats staggered while they attempted to regain their sight.

Can't we track them? panted Duncan, shielding his eyes.

Amiri shook his head. *There are too many scents above ground to track them without causing notice. Dukatt knew that when he sent them through this tunnel.* Amiri kicked the concrete with his paw. *They could be anywhere. We have lost... the colony is lost.* His eyes suddenly flashed with a frightening realization. *They will know how to find us now. The purebreds will come after us under the cover of dark. We must move while we have time.*

Duncan was staring in disbelief into the distance.

Can you manage? Amiri asked Duncan urgently.

Duncan said nothing. Whiski turned to Amiri. She replied. *We can manage.*

Amiri stared solemnly at Duncan. *I hope we meet again someday, Son of Sagira.*

Thank you, Amiri, whispered Whiski, *for all that you did, and all that you tried to do.* She bowed to the feral leader. *My real name is Whiski; this is Duncan. We live just a couple blocks down south of here on Olive Street. If you ever need us...* her voice trailed off.

Amiri smiled sadly. *Well, it has been a great honor, Whiski and Duncan.*

Where will you go? asked Duncan, finding his voice.

We will find our way. There are other copies of the book to protect. We will seek them out.

Amiri put his paw on each of their foreheads in an ancient goodbye. *May Sagira protect and watch over you.*

Duncan stuck out his paw to grab Amiri who had turned to jump back into the sewers.

I... I am so sorry, Amiri. All of this is my fault.

Amiri sighed sadly. *The Children of Sagira bring death and destruction with them wherever they go. Yours is both a gift and a curse. It is who you are.* He gave a pained smile. *There is no changing that, even after all this time.*

And with those heavy words, Amiri faded away into the blackness of the sewer.

~

When he had made it deep into the tunnels, he found his daughter still breathing heavily and waiting for him. *Father, I lost them...*

Amiri placed his paw on Nafisa's. *I know.*

I am so sorry, Father. I have failed our clan.

No daughter, I have failed them.

Nafisa's ears fell back in surprise. *What is it, father?*

Amiri looked hard at his daughter. *I have something to tell you, child. The book stolen from us was not the real Book of Sagira.*

Nafisa's face fell. *What are you saying, father?*

Amiri sighed and hung his head. *There is only one true copy left remaining in this world, and it is not we who guard it. The last record of the words of Sagira is in the paws of the purebreds.*

Chapter 29

Whiski had to bark orders into Duncan's ear to keep him moving toward home. She tried to keep them in the shadows, but it was early morning, and the shadows were shrinking. They needed to keep moving. Fortunately, the winding tunnels had placed them only a few blocks from home. Whiski recognized the houses as part of their neighborhood.

Duncan moved forward, but his eyes were empty. The words of his mother, spoken by Amiri, kept echoing in his mind. I am destruction, pain, and death. I am cursed, he thought to himself. My mother knew all along. She was trying to tell me, but I thought I knew better. I thought I could fix things and everything would be all right. Duncan was absorbed in his own dark thoughts so much so that only Whiski's voice really seemed to cut through the weight of it all and keep him going. He kept whispering, *I am Sagira... my fate is hers.*

Dunkelberry, don't you stop. We're not home yet, Mister, keep marching! She kept butting him forward with her head. There was no way she could carry him alone, so she did what she could to keep him moving, to keep him safe. She had to stop multiple times to pull them into bushes whenever a car passed by or she heard human voices.

When they reached the house, Whiski scanned the backyard for signs of Franklin or his sister, but it was deserted. She dragged Duncan to the base of the window, jumped up and wedged her claws in the crack she had left. She heaved and pushed it open, then jumped down. Duncan resisted her. *No, I'm not safe. I can't.* He kept repeating these words to her, but Whiski yelled and clawed and bit until Duncan jumped through and collapsed on the ground of their familiar kitchen floor.

Duncan, listen to me. I need to you to drink or eat something.

Duncan shook his head. *Sleep.*

Fine, you can sleep, but after you have something to drink and I clean you up first, okay?

Duncan nodded. He felt as helpless as a newborn kitten again. *It's lost, Whiski, it's all lost.*

Whiski managed to coax and then drag Duncan into the human sink. They were both filthy, but he even more so as he had had to continually cover himself in mud and sewage to keep the fire at bay on their journey. Whiski turned on the water so that it was cool. She cupped her paw and began slowly washing the dirt and grime out of his fur. Duncan's voice was slurred. He was slipping into unconsciousness. *I don't want to hurt you. I don't want to hurt you, Whiski.*

Whiski stroked his ears with her paws. *You'll feel better once you get all of this off, kid.* Duncan's usually bright yellow eyes were a muted dark gold, as he stared sadly off into the distance.

Once he was washed clean, and the water no longer ran any shade of brown, Whiski held him close to her and began to dry him with her tongue. As she did this, she purred a soft lullaby her mother had once sung to her. She sang until Duncan, Son of Sagira, fell asleep in her arms.

Sleep, little kitten

Let yourself fall

Sagira won't find you

Not while I stand tall

Sleep, little kitten

The world can wait

No matter what happens

I'll be here you when you wake

Chapter 30

You do realize that it's daylight now, don't you?

Yes, I'm sorry, Varik. It was difficult to convince her to come. Franklin had his orange tail wrapped around Vera's shoulders. *She is not well.*

My humans will be awake in a few hours. We do not have long.

Vera? said Varik in a smooth, hypnotic voice. *Vera, I am Varik. Do you remember me?*

Vera kept shaking her head.

Do you remember who did this to you?

Vera started backing away from Varik. Franklin tried to comfort her. *It's okay, Sister. He is here to help.*

Silence, purred Varik in that same silky voice he was using with Vera. *Tell me what you do remember, Vera, dear. You are safe here, child. Speak,* coaxed Varik reassuringly.

Colors, reds and oranges, Vera's eyes were blinking rapidly, *I remember light, blinding light, and then... then nothing but darkness.*

She's beginning to remember things, Varik, interrupted Franklin.

How many times must I ask you to be silent, Franklin?

Franklin went immediately quiet. Varik glared at him and then turned his jewel-like green eyes back toward Vera. He sighed. *She will never be the same, Franklin.*

But Varik... I thought you could help her. I thought...

There is damage here that cannot be undone. She is beyond my aid. Vera will be like this for the rest of her life, a fearful kitten, scared, confused, and innocent. You must take her back to her humans.

No! blurted Franklin.

Varik rose up to his full height. His eyes were fixed on Franklin.

Hello? Varik?

All three cats turned to see where this new voice was coming from. A young ginger cat and her marbled tabby brother stood in the window. The brother was holding a small black book attached to a strap. The pair looked nervous and exhausted.

Franklin thought he had never seen anything so peculiar. Ferals above ground! And looking for Varik no less!

Varik's hackles immediately went up. He was a naturally imposing figure, but when he was surprised, he could become simply terrifying. *State your purpose!*

The ginger girl bowed. *I am Aissa. This is my brother, Jabari. We are children of Dukatt, member of the feral council of Haji. We come looking to trade.*

Varik's hackles went down, but he remained large and imposing in the morning light.

You come to trade at a poor time of day, spoke Varik suspiciously. He eyed the book the tomcat was carrying. The girl was still breathing fast. They'd clearly been running.

We seek sanctuary above ground. Aissa nodded at her brother who then hopped down and presented Varik with the book by laying it at his feet.

Varik looked down with narrowed eyes at Jabari. *Is this what I think it is?*

Yes. The tomcat bowed his head. *The Book of Sagira, our colony's only copy.*

This is quite a rare item for two young ferals to obtain. How did you come by this? questioned Varik coolly.

Jabari looked nervously at Aissa. Aissa spoke confidently. *Our father sent us here with the book in exchange for our safety.*

Varik tilted his head and examined the girl cat. *The ferals would not part with this lightly.*

Aissa paused and exchanged a long look with her brother. *We forced their hand. We exchanged the book for two imposters, one posing as a Son of Sagira and the other, as his servant.*

Varik's ears flicked forward. He accepted the book, trying not to reveal his excitement.

By any chance, was this pair a young black tomcat and an older black-and-white female missing part of her tail?

240

Franklin's head rose sharply in surprise.

Yes, replied Aissa cautiously. *But of course they were imposters.*

Yes, yes, of course, agreed Varik calmly. And after a slight pause, *Do you know where they are now?*

Likely still with the colony, answered Jabari. Aissa shot her brother a harsh look.

Varik frowned sympathetically, *But you of course are no longer with the colony. Is that not right?*

Aissa and Jabari nodded.

Varik looked over at Franklin and Vera and then back to the two ferals standing in his basement.

I will grant you sanctuary for the book, but with one other condition. I wish you to lead some of my guards to your former colony.

Jabari started to object, but Aissa shook her head. *It seems we have no other choice.*

Excellent! There is a Siamese who lives in a large white home with a stone fountain five houses south of here. You will find her out on the back porch this time of day. Tell her I wish her to gather four other guards. You are to take them to the colony at first dark. Do you understand?

Aissa bowed slightly. *Yes,* she spoke through gritted teeth.

Good. There is a park several blocks west from here. Do you know it?

The female cat nodded.

You and your brother may live out your years there. You are under the protection of my guard should you need it. Varik's lips couldn't help but curl up in a dark smile as he spoke the last part.

That's it? asked Jabari. His sister gave him a warning look. Jabari glared in response but said nothing. He rejoined his sister in the open window, and they left without saying another word.

Varik turned to Franklin. *Call a meeting for early tomorrow morning.* He was staring eagerly at the book lying on the floor in front of them.

But Varik, my sister needs...

I told you nothing can be done! Take her back to her humans! You test my patience today, Franklin. She has served the guard well. Leave her in peace.

What about the mixed-breeds? Did they do this to her?

Varik hissed, *All in good time. Go immediately! I am tired of your constant whining. My humans will be awake soon.*

Franklin frowned but obediently turned with his sister to leave, his tail still curled protectively around her shoulders.

After you return Vera and deliver my message, I have one more task for you.

Yes, Varik?

I want you to resume your watch over the mixed-breeds. I expect they will be returning home soon, and when they do, report immediately back to me. Immediately. I am counting on you, Franklin.

Yes, Varik.

And, Franklin?

Yes, Varik?

Leave your sister home from now on. There is nothing more she can do for the guard.

Franklin nodded and gently assisted Vera back out through the window.

Or for me, Varik whispered as he watched them leave.

Chapter 31

Duncan stirred restlessly in his sleep. He could see fire all around them. Their house was in flames. He could hear the humans crying out, but he couldn't see them. Whiski lay trapped in the fire. She was calling out his name, but all he could say was, *I'm sorry! I'm sorry!* He could see their food and water bowls melting from the heat and the pictures of the young couple cracking and curling inward from the fire. Duncan looked down. He was on fire, too! This was his fault! This was all his fault! Duncan woke up yowling and panting for breath.

Whiski ran back into the kitchen. *What on Earth? What's wrong?*

Duncan stared hard at Whiski. The image of her dying in the blackened rubble was burned into his brain. *Nothing, just a bad dream.* Duncan shook his head. He felt like he needed to sleep for a week. He jumped down beside her.

You look awful.

Thanks, you too.

Whiski gestured. *Come on, it's breakfast time, or I guess it's human brunch time. It's nearly noon.*

Duncan nodded. He could barely remember their trip home after exiting the sewer.

The two cats munched silently next to one another. Duncan realized Whiski's tail fur was slightly singed.

Are you okay? He nearly choked on his kibble. *You didn't tell me you were hurt!*

Whiski brushed off his concern. *I'm fine, Dunkelberry. I have very little tail left anyway. The fur just got a little burnt when we were...* she didn't continue the sentence, she didn't have to.

Duncan took a step back. *I could have killed you.*

Whiski exhaled heavily. *Calm down, kid. That was an unusual situation. Now that we're home, you've got the sink, and all kinds of ways to cool down fast.*

Duncan shook his head. *No, I'm dangerous. You were right. You shouldn't be around me.*

Listen, kid, I made the decision to stick it out with you when we stepped outside this house together for the first time last night. She paused to look at Duncan seriously for a moment. *We're family, Duncan. We take care of each other.*

No, we're not! growled Duncan. *You said so yourself.*

Whiski's voice rose in frustration. *I know I said that, but we are. I mean, we're family! Besides,* she paused, changing tactics, *only family can be this truly annoying!*

When Duncan didn't smile, she let out an exasperated sigh. *Stop worrying about me, and get ahold of yourself! You're ruining brunch.*

Duncan frowned at Whiski but continued to say nothing.

Both cats' ears flicked back at the surprise sound of a key in the door.

We're back early! shouted the human woman's voice. She scooped up Duncan and started kissing him while he struggled to break free, and then grabbed Whiski and did the same. They went through a similar, but thankfully shorter, ordeal with the human man but were forced to sit without talking while their humans unpacked.

The day went slowly. Duncan spent most of it staring despondently out the bedroom window at the melting snow while Whiski spent it apprehensively watching Duncan. The humans turned both heaters up and gave each cat a hug before going to bed late that evening.

Neither cat noticed the orange Persian watching from outside their window.

No matter what Duncan did, he couldn't get that image of Whiski in the fire out of his mind. Was this her fate if he stayed here? He thought of his mother's words. *There is always a cost to choosing a different path.* He looked at Whiski and frowned.

Whiski waited to approach him until the humans were snoring softly.

You've been spending all day staring out this bedroom window.

Duncan sighed but said nothing.

Duncan, I want to talk to you.

Duncan looked forlornly at Whiski. *You used my real name, it must be serious.*

Whiski gave him a small smirk. *I've been thinking about what Amiri said to you.*

Duncan nodded grimly. *Me too.*

Duncan, you may never be a normal house cat.

Duncan rolled over onto his back to show her his flickering hind leg. *No really, ya think?*

Whiski pretended to ignore him and continued. *But Duncan, you are not cursed. You won't destroy everything you touch.*

Duncan snorted. *Yeah, maybe not everything, just almost everything... the toaster may survive.*

Duncan, shut up, I'm trying to say something here.

Duncan rolled his eyes but stayed quiet.

Here's the thing. When I met you, before I found what you were... I was still scared of you.

Duncan cocked his whiskers skeptically, but listened as Whiski continued.

I know, I know, me, afraid of you. Minus your ability to burst into flames and mess with other cats' minds, you're about as scary as a show poodle. But here's the thing... I realized while we were out with the ferals last night that I didn't want you to be a part of this family because I was afraid if I had to care about anyone again, I'd only end up losing them. Whiski paused and sighed painfully. *Losing my brother nearly killed me, and I didn't think I could go through that again. But when you walked into this house, all of that went away. I couldn't avoid you. You wouldn't let me. And then, I found out who you really were...*

Duncan turned to stare back out the window. *You mean, a Child of Sagira, who destroys everything he touches?*

No... Whiski stopped, *I thought I told you to shut up. Duncan, I realized that you were a strong, brave, kind tomcat, and I saw that my world would never be the same without you. You're my best friend, as sad as that is,* Whiski shifted uncomfortably. *It's the truth.* When Duncan didn't speak, she continued. *Friendships and family are all about knowing the risks, facing them, and choosing to be there anyway.* Duncan shook his head, but Whiski kept going. *And yeah, you may not have everything figured out yet, and yeah, I know you're probably scared out of your mind with what's been happening to you, but it's going to be okay. We will figure it out. And you, Duncan, Son of Sagira, will be okay. You know why? Because you don't have to go through any of this by yourself. I'm here. I believe in you, Duncan, and I trust you. Now I need you to trust me.*

Duncan shook his head. *You know, when I was a kitten, I actually wanted to be special.* He paused and rubbed his tired face with his paws. *But the thing you don't think about when you're little is that being special means being different... and being different means being alone.* Duncan swallowed hard. *And no matter how hard you try, you can't be like everyone else, because deep down, you are different, and you always will be.* Whiski tried to interrupt, but Duncan held up a weary black paw. *When I found out what I was, everything changed.* He looked hard at Whiski. *I didn't want to be special anymore.* He looked dejectedly back out the window. *The funny thing is that I thought.... you know, I really thought I could hide that part of me from the world, leave it in the past while I moved on. But Whiski, I was wrong. Wherever I go, Sagira goes with me. You know I trust you. There's no* one else in this world I trust more. *I wish I could believe you when you say that everything is going to be okay, but as long as I'm here, I'm a danger to you and our humans.*

Stop it! Whiski shook her head in frustration. *You are a good cat, Duncan. You learned to control your sight, you can learn to control the other powers! I know, deep down, that you would never do anything to hurt me or our humans. That's enough for me, kid. I don't care how much ancient Sagira blood you have running through that fat tomcat body of yours. You don't need an ancient book to tell you what kind of life you can lead!* She punched his shoulder softly with her paw. *You have me to do that for you!*

Duncan realized what he had to do. He loved Whiski, and because of that, he needed to run to save her. He turned and let his heavy golden eyes meet hers.

Whiski, Duncan whispered. *Go to sleep.*

And she did.

Duncan paused to whisper something in her ear. He kissed her gently on the head. *If this is the price I have to pay, then so be it.* He pushed open the kitchen window and then, without looking back, he disappeared into the night.

Chapter 32

It was three in the morning, and the purebreds were filing into Varik's basement. For a meeting to be called outside the usual schedule was extremely rare, and as such, the basement was whirring with anticipation. In fact, only Franklin seemed sullen and preoccupied. Several cats stopped to ask him where his sister was, but he refused to speak to them. Once they had all arrived, Varik moved forward and asked for silence. He pushed the leather book forward to the center of the circle. *We have in our possession,* he paused for dramatic effect, *a copy of the Book of Sagira.*

The purebreds gasped.

We gather here tonight to destroy what has symbolized so much destruction and terror for our kind for centuries. We gather here tonight to end a piece of history that has threatened our very species. We gather here, living proof, that there are still honorable cats willing to sacrifice much to keep our kind safe.

But, there is more, Varik smiled.

The purebreds looked quizzically at one another. What else could there possibly be?

Rose, Varik pointed to a young Siamese with large blue eyes, *was sent with a team to investigate a nearby feral colony, the same feral colony that has given us this book!*

What did you find, Rose? asked Varik smugly.

Rose stepped forward. *I found nothing, Varik. The colony has fled.*

Varik smiled. *You see, they finally understood that to defy us was to defy all good and honest cats. And so, out of fear and shame, they have finally fled our territory! We have outsmarted and outlasted them.*

Many of the cats murmured noises of approval, or nodded their heads to show their support.

But let us stop to remember why we do so. I have grave news to tell you all. News that saddens me so that it darkens what should be a glorious night. Franklin's dear sister, Vera, has been attacked and blinded by a Child of Sagira.

Intense whispers and gasps filled the room. *No! How can it be? I thought they were just fairy tales to scare kittens! Their kind is supposed to be dead. Here, in our territory?*

Silence! Varik's commanding voice ascended above the group and they fell completely silent.

I have determined where this cat lives. And tonight, brothers and sisters, we shall destroy not only the Book of Sagira, but one of her children as well. We shall end this reign of terror and destruction. We shall not let a Child of Sagira continue to attack us without cause! We shall take back the present from this demon birthed in the past!

The slender Siamese raised her paw.

Yes, Rose?

How shall we accomplish this noble task, Varik?

Varik smiled. *This is a child of sight, and you shall destroy both the cat and the book in the ways of old. With fire, Rose, with fire. Quickly, before the beast can escape! Franklin tells me that the two cats have returned home. You will strike tonight!*

Varik let his voice drop to a fevered whisper. *Now listen closely while I explain to you what must be done.*

Chapter 33

Duncan found himself walking the same path that they followed the previous night. He wasn't sure where he was headed exactly. He stopped and paused to listen at the sound of every snapped twig. He couldn't help but feel like he was being followed. Duncan shook his head and picked up his pace so that he was moving at a slow run. He knew he needed to keep moving as quickly as possible before Whiski woke up. Duncan sighed. She would never forgive him for this. Duncan smiled grimly, at least she would be alive to hate him.

Duncan moved to hide under a stretch of bushes. Where could he go? He couldn't go back to his mother. He was sure of that. Duncan stared out into the night. He couldn't risk going back to the ferals either.

It was as his mother had said. He must walk alone. But instead of walking, he sat terrified, looking out into the unknown, not sure in which direction to head. It's one thing to choose a path in life; it is quite another to walk it, he thought to himself. Gathering his courage, he picked his body up to head north when a vision struck him so hard he fell to the ground. His body seized and his limbs contracted.

Fire... flashes of yellows and reds. The fire was burning their house again. But he'd left, how could the fire still be happening? He could hear the humans screaming. There were other faces now, cats sneering and hissing. The colors in the fire mixed together and made their faces look demonic in the red light. Duncan could see Whiski fighting them off, but she had been badly slashed by one of the cats and one of her legs looked broken.

Duncan's body lurched violently. *We are the guard, you mixed-breed trash! Varik has sent us to make sure you never hurt another one of us again! You will pay for your sins!* yowled a slender Siamese with ice-blue eyes. *Where is the tomcat! Where is the son of sight?* She turned to yell at the eyes Duncan was seeing through. *Franklin, you said they were both still here!*

Duncan fought the vision, trying to pull himself back out of it, but he was in too deep, and the fire was too hot. Whiski lay dying in the burning rubble. She closed her eyes and spoke his name.

They were going to kill his whole family! His mother's words echoed in his mind. *Hate lives on long after love dies.*

He wasn't there to protect them. What had he done?

The vision flashed forward, and he could see Franklin's frightened face staring back at him from the reflection in the glass windows. Vera cried as she held her brother and the vision shattered along with the glass...

No!

Duncan wheeled around on the grass, tearing out large chunks as he changed directions. He did not see the pair of feral green eyes, outlined in black, that watched him, bewildered, from the gutter.

Duncan began running as fast as he possibly could toward home. How would he ever make it? He pushed faster and faster until it felt like he was barely touching the ground. The fifth power exploded out of his body like a rocket. He felt it surge as he fought against the vision of flames and death. Duncan's legs drove forward in perfect time as he ran. He felt her ancient power pressing against his golden eyes and pulling on his mind. He felt her fire coursing through his blood. He watched her veiled darkness melt into his fur. But he held the fifth power in his heart as it pounded and beat through his paws into the ground.

Duncan felt Sagira as he pressed his body into the black wind that swept across the night sky, and he let her carry him home.

~

Duncan skidded to a stop several blocks from his home. He could see the flames against the night sky. Vera, the brown Persian, stood blocking the narrow path between the hedges that separated Duncan from his family. She held up her paw to stop him.

Duncan bared his fangs. *Let me pass,* he growled!

Vera remained motionless, blinking at Duncan. *You must not die, Son of Sagira. You must see. There is no time.*

My friend is in there! Let me go, move! Duncan raised his body up and unsheathed his claws. *Move out of my way, or I will move you myself!*

Vera stayed still, shaking her head and staring plaintively at Duncan.

255

Fine! Duncan shoved Vera to the ground and took off toward his burning home.

Vera watched the fire sadly from the ground. *You must see,* she whispered to the empty night.

Chapter 34

Varik hunkered down in the cold air and the wet patches of snow. He held the Book of Sagira by its strap. He had to move quickly. He had orders to deliver the book to a cat he'd never met, but he knew she was higher up in the guard. Varik shook his head. He had thought they would have wanted it destroyed, but his contact had specifically told him to bring it to this location and tell no one. He had given his guard a small journal of his human's to destroy instead. Having never seen the Book of Sagira, they would not be suspicious, Varik was sure of it. They trusted him, and Varik had felt a momentary pang of guilt for lying to them, but he had his orders. Besides, it was time for him take his rightful place in the elite guard. He lowered the book to the ground and pushed it under the boughs of the holly bush.

A voice whispered out of the darkness. *Do you bleed the blood that is pure?*

Varik bowed his head and held out his paw. *Yes, I bleed the blood that is pure.*

He looked up to see a Turkish Angora staring coldly back at him. *You have done well, brother,* she whispered. *We had thought there were no more left.*

Varik bowed and licked the blood from his paw.

The Turkish Angora opened the book and raised her head sharply. *What is this?* She hissed. *What are you playing at?*

At first Varik was at a loss for words. He was not used to being treated this way. He growled defensively. *Two ferals, they brought it to me! They traded it for their safety!*

You lie! The journal is a fake!

No, growled Varik! *There is a Son of Sagira, a child born of sight, my guard attacks him now!*

You have been played for a fool, Varik. The Turkish Angora narrowed her eyes. She had one blue and one green. Both were cold. *And if you have truly lost a child of sight tonight, you will answer to the head of the guard for this.* She hissed into his face and disappeared into the night.

~

Franklin and the five other purebreds who had volunteered were huddled outside of the mixed-breeds' house. Rose the Siamese, Ivan the Russian Blue, Roan the Devon Rex, Adair the Manx, and Ming the Tonkinese.

Franklin fumed. To think that they were the ones who attacked them that night! He would make both the girl and the tomcat pay. Tonight was for Vera. He caught a glimpse of his reflection in the window. Franklin shook his head, trying to rid himself of doubt. If revenge was the only way he could help her, then he would do what the guard required of him.

Rose carried what she believed to be the book of Sagira in her teeth and nodded at Franklin. She dragged its bottom carelessly across the ground. Franklin looked up at Roan and Ivan. They signaled that all was clear. Franklin pushed open the cracked back window and signaled for the other cats to follow quickly. Neither mixed-breed was anywhere to be seen. They must be in the bedroom with their humans, Franklin thought to himself. The other purebreds began tearing out pages of the book and stuffing them into the floor vents. They began to crackle and glow in the heaters, and then like a firecracker, sparks began shooting out of the vents. As the sparks fell, they lit everything in their path ablaze. The flames licked across the carpet quickly.

Whiski's eyes snapped open. Her head was throbbing. She smelled smoke. What was happening? Whiski bolted up and turned her ears and nose every which way to determine the location of the threat. The last thing she remembered was talking to Duncan and him telling her to go to sleep... Whiski cursed aloud to herself, realizing what he had done. But the fire, she saw the glow of the flames and the smoke beginning to billow into the bedroom. She heard Franklin's voice. Growling, Whiski jumped down from the bed and tried to steady herself. Her body was heavy and off-balance. She let loose a guttural yowl loud enough to wake her humans. She could hear the woman screaming and then the man immediately yelling out for her and Duncan. They called to her, but she shook her head. If Duncan was gone, then he was safe. Her humans were safe. They could escape through the front windows. That was all that mattered. She took off running into the growing fire.

Franklin! What are you doing? demanded Whiski.

259

Rose knocked her flat on her face from behind. One of the other purebreds gave a swift kick to her back leg, snapping the bone.

We are the guard, you mixed-breed trash! Varik has sent us to make sure you never hurt another one of us again! You will pay for your sins! She yowled. *Where is the tomcat? Where is the child of sight!*

Franklin, you said they were both here! threatened the Siamese.

Franklin grabbed Whiski's ears and held her face to the fire.

Which one of you hurt my sister? yelled Franklin.

The smoke began to thicken. It was getting harder to breathe. The heat was almost unbearable. Roan and Ming had already run away. Adair and Ivan continued to rip out chunks of the book of Sagira and toss the pages into the fire.

Whiski choked as she spoke. *What do you mean?* It was getting harder to yell. Whiski blinked hard.

Rose hissed menacingly. *We want the Son of Sagira!*

Well, you can't have him! Your fight ends with me. Whiski lunged at Franklin, but she was outnumbered and weakened by the smoke and her injured leg. Rose sliced down her forearm, leaving a two-inch wound that opened up the muscle underneath her skin. Whiski screamed in pain. Franklin staggered back, frightened.

Adair and Ivan abandoned what was left of the torn book and pinned Whiski's good leg with debris while Rose held her by her neck, but not before Whiski left several deep gashes on her face.

To remember me by, she growled, laughing as the Siamese clutched her lacerated cheek.

Rose hit Whiski hard across the face in disgust one last time, and then turned to escape with the rest of the purebreds. Franklin didn't move.

Whiski looked hard at him, *If he dies, so does any chance of helping your sister.*

Rose pulled at Franklin, *Our work here is done. The tomcat has fled! We must go! Now! The building is giving way.*

What did she say? Franklin pressed forward, resisting Rose. His voice cracked in the heat as he yelled back at Whiski. *Can you help her? Can you help my sister?*

We need to get out of here, yelled Rose.

Rose pulled on Franklin. He looked at Whiski reluctantly and then, hesitating, he turned and ran. He cleared the window just as a beam fell and splintered on the ground, causing the flames to rise even higher.

Several minutes passed for Whiski alone in the burning building. She could hear the human woman screaming outside for her and Duncan. She was slipping in and out of consciousness. Soon... she thought to herself... soon it'll all be over.

Whiski! a familiar voice rose above the roaring flames. *Whiski!*

Whiski looked up, and though her vision was starting to cloud, she could see him. It was Duncan, wreathed in fire.

Chapter 35

Whiski! I'm sorry! I'm so sorry! Duncan rushed through the burning house, trying to get to the place he had seen in his vision. *Where are you?*

A hunk of drywall fell and hurled the burning counterfeit Book of Sagira into the air. Crackling, it landed on what remained of the kitchen table.

Here! Duncan could hear her voice struggling against the smoke and flames. *Duncan, I'm here.*

The ravaged book lay on one side of the burning room and Whiski lay pinned on the other. Scorched pages were falling like fiery rain in the hot air. Duncan could see the familiar leather cover hanging off the kitchen table as it burned...

His mother's words came back to him. *We walk alone.* Duncan shook his head defiantly and growled at the walls of fire. *Not anymore.* He dove through the blaze after Whiski and shoved the debris off her badly beaten body. Breathing into the fire, his flames went out around his muzzle and he gently lifted Whiski by the neck. Dragging her as carefully as he could, Duncan ran backward through the rippling tides of heat, shielding her with his body. He winced as shards of glass from the shattered sliding-glass door pierced his paws.

Duncan set Whiski down gently in the cool, snow-covered grass and began licking her face. The flames that covered his body went out almost instantly.

She was unconscious.

Duncan buried his face in her fur. *Whiski! Whiski, don't go! I'm sorry! I was trying to save you by leaving. I didn't know. I didn't see. I told you I would protect you, and I... I broke my promise to you. I... I...* Hot tears trickled down Duncan's face and evaporated before they left his muzzle. *I'll never leave you again, just please wake up. Whiski, please don't leave me.*

Whiski's eyes opened slowly. *Dunkelberry? Is that you?*

Duncan's head snapped up. *Whiski?*

Whiski blinked hard, trying to figure out if what she was seeing was real. *Why are you crying like a three-week-old kitten?* She coughed.

Duncan hugged her but stopped when she flinched. *Are you okay?*

Whiski was breathing heavily. *Barely, kid. Glad you came back.* She flashed a sooty grin at Duncan. *I love you too. Now get off me,* she wheezed, *you're hot.*

Suddenly, remembering the book, she gasped and weakly grabbed his paw. *The book, the book is still inside! You have to go back!*

Duncan shook his head. *We need to get you to the humans. You need to see a doctor. Can you walk?*

Whiski shook her head painfully, then smiled at Duncan. *You should've seen the other guy...*

Duncan gently brushed her forehead with his paw. *Stay here, I'll be right back.* He ran quickly around to the side of the house, leaving a trail of bloody paw prints in the snow. Duncan sighed in relief when he spotted a firefighter. He approached the large man and met his eyes, *Come here, hurry,* he whispered. The fireman stopped what he was doing and began running after Duncan. He was a large, burly man with bushy black eyebrows, and his gear was covered in ash from the blaze. He blinked several times and looked around him as though he was lost. Duncan meowed and the firefighter finally looked down at the two cats. He spoke soothing words as he bent to the ground and carefully scooped up Whiski. She seemed so small and fragile cradled in the big man's arms. He lifted Duncan in the other arm, and they were soon reunited in front of the burning house with their humans. The woman, red-eyed, had already been weeping, but she cried harder when she saw Whiski. The man ran a finger gently over Whiski's burned whiskers. Together, the little family watched as what was left of their house crumbled to the ground. Duncan could see the relief and pain in the couple's eyes as they held both cats and carefully examined Whiski's broken body and his lacerated paws.

Duncan turned his head to look at the blackened remains of his home, and his body went rigid. He saw four purebreds sitting out in their yards defiantly watching his house burn. He had seen their faces in his vision; he had memorized their features. He looked for Franklin and Vera, but they were nowhere to be found. Duncan's eyes flashed a brilliant gold in the morning light. He wanted them to see him alive. He wanted them to know that he and Whiski had both survived... but most of all, he wanted them to understand that he was a Son of Sagira, and he knew that they were the ones who had attacked his family.

Feeling Duncan's angry golden eyes lock onto theirs, the remaining members of the guard scattered in silence, seeking the sanctuary of their respective houses. While Duncan watched them run, he could feel himself being lifted into a waiting car with Whiski. As the firefighters continued to battle the fire, Duncan turned away and began to gently groom Whiski's ears. His family was safe, and from now on he would always be there to protect them. He would master the five powers of Sagira, and he would use them without mercy against any who dared to threaten his family. If he searched for answers about Sagira, he would search with Whiski by his side.

He was different, and he would always be different, but for the first time in his life, Duncan, Son of Sagira, knew that whatever path fate had laid out for him, he would never have to walk it alone.

A Preview of Book Two in the Duncan Trilogy

900 B.C., in a lonely stretch of Egyptian desert

Sagira quickened her pace. No matter how hard she tried, she could never outrun the images that burned like wildfire through her mind. For some time now, these images--these fragments of lives that were not her own--had grown in strength until they were all that she could see.

Sagira narrowed her eyes. She had seen what her children would become. She had seen the darkness and the pain that would follow them. But nothing, nothing had prepared her for what would happen, what had to happen, once she saw *him*.

He must survive. Sagira shook her head in desperation and thought aloud to herself. *He must see.* She pushed forward, her dark body seamless against the night. Sagira skidded to a stop in front of a small cave, pausing to study the entrance. She had been here before, not in the flesh, but her eyes knew the spot well. There was a small break in the rocks, only about a foot across. She ran her small black paw over the familiar opening and breathed deeply. The night air still retained the oppressive heat of the sun, but even then, it felt cool against her tired face. Under the cover of darkness, the animals that made the desert their home were at their most active. They hunted and scavenged in the night, and they were utterly preoccupied with their own survival. Sagira sat quietly, listening to the humming of creatures moving about in the solitary darkness. She was born a child of the desert and to the desert she would return. Her actions tonight would set into motion a series of

267

events that must come to pass. Yes, this was the path she must walk. This was the only way she could help him. She had seen it.

As Sagira began to move forward, a small mouse came scurrying out of the cave. She jumped back in surprise. There were so few things that had the power to surprise her anymore. For a moment, the two creatures stared at one another. Instinct told Sagira to kill it, but instead she watched with stunned curiosity as its small body shook with fear. Eyeing the dark predator, the mouse cautiously took a step forward. Sagira did nothing. The mouse's chest heaved and its eyes darted warily back and forth. Not fully understanding why it was still alive, but realizing that it must act, the mouse took off running into the night. Sagira smiled thoughtfully, pausing to look up into the night sky. *A curious thing to see so much and yet miss something so small,* she mused to herself.

Flashing her golden eyes, Sagira covered her body in flames. Moving like a torch into the cave, she let her light burn down until her eyes were all that shone against the deep blackness. She had seen herself walking down this path so many times. She could have moved through the darkness with her eyes closed. When she came to the end of the path, she laid herself down on the cool stone and closed her eyes, extinguishing her light for the last time. Sagira gently placed her head on her paws and waited for the life to leave her body. *I will die alone,* she whispered sadly to the empty cave, *but I have always been alone.*

Sagira could hear another animal breathing and the sound of its body shifting against the stone floor. She raised her head sharply, her golden eyes fixed on the shadowy corner across from her. She was not alone. How could anyone have followed her? She had been so careful. She unsheathed her claws and flattened her ears against her head. She set her body ablaze and prepared to attack. Against her light, Sagira could see the outline of his black body. She took a step forward to examine his face. *How?* Her ears came forward and her expression softened as she recognized him. She shook her head in disbelief. Her flames died out, shrouding them both in darkness. *I did not see you coming.* Slowly, Sagira lowered her body back down. *Thank you, child,* she whispered. *Thank you for waiting with me.* Closing her eyes, she could feel him fading away into the darkness. Smiling, she spoke softly, answering a question only she could hear. *Duncan, my son, this is the way it must end.*

About the Author

The daughter of a librarian and a professor, E.C. Holley grew up surrounded by books. As time passed, her belief in the power of story-telling only grew stronger. Fascinated by the mysterious life of house cats, she drew inspiration from her much loved feline companions and began building a world of cats filled with ancient powers, purebred guards, and feral clans. Duncan, Son of Sagira is the first in a series of books dedicated to the mysterious Children of Sagira.

E.C. Holley is an Assistant Professor of Management at Central Washington University, and she currently lives in Kirkland, Washington, with her computer programmer husband and her two (seriously unimpressed) cats.

For more information about E.C. Holley and her Children of Sagira series, check out her website at www.sonofsagira.com!

Duncan, Son of Sagira is illustrated by artist, Laura E. Penn, who currently lives in Akron, New York with her husband, two sons, two dogs, and a "Son of Sagira" who goes by the name of Chad.

Acknowledgments

First, I want to thank my husband, Brian Holley, for his constant love and support throughout this journey of writing and publishing this novel. I also want to thank my sister, Laura, for her beautiful illustrations that brought *Duncan, Son of Sagira* to life, and my brother-in-law, Brian R., for his brilliant photo editing. I want to give a huge thank you to my marketing agent and dear friend, Noelle, as well as my copy editor, Daniel, for all the time and energy they've spent helping me prepare this novel for publication. I also want to thank my family and friends that have given me courage to pursue my passion, and especially those of you that read the many drafts of this novel and watched it transform from an inspiration into a manuscript. Brian H., Mom, Maggie, Laura, Anna R., Brian R., Jude, Kristen, Danielle, Dan, Noelle, and Adrian, thank you so much for reading my novel. But most of all, I want to thank the cats in my life that have served as my muses throughout this entire process. A life without you would be an empty one. Thank you for taking this journey with me.

Made in the USA
San Bernardino, CA
22 November 2013